The Sunshine Potluck Society

SUNSHINE SERIES
BOOK ONE

LILLY MIRREN

For my Mum...

Chapter One

The sweet scent of golden corn and heady aroma of cilantro wove its way through the air and around Joanna's head as she bent over the hot open oven door. She breathed in deep, then shut the door again. It would be ready soon, and she couldn't wait for the guests to arrive. Corn off the cob and refried beans dusted with grated cheese were only two of the dishes that she'd be serving at this month's potluck. There was also shredded pork, Mexican rice and an assortment of fresh salads to go with their Mexican theme.

She smiled at Emily, her in-home carer and unofficial sous-chef who was frying tortillas in an electric pan on the other side of the kitchen island.

"How's it going over there?"

Emily tucked a strand of her long, straight brown hair behind her ear. Her brow creased. "I think...good. I'm not sure. Do you want to take a look?"

Joanna strode around the outside of the island, lifted the edge of the foil, and studied the pile of tortillas on a large plate. "They look great. You're doing a fantastic job. Well done, Sous-Chef!"

Emily grinned with pride. "Thanks, Chef."

The monthly gathering of what Joanna impulsively called the *Sunshine Potluck Society* had become a staple in her life. In fact, it was more than a staple. It *was* her life. Her children had moved away years earlier, and they were busy with their careers and families. When Ron passed a decade ago, she'd taken to spending more and more of her time indoors until finally, three years ago, she realised she hadn't stepped a foot outside of her front yard in six months.

These days, she tried to go somewhere once a month, but the effort usually left her feeling worn out. And she much preferred to stay in. It was safe in her home, warm and cozy. She ordered her groceries online, and just about anything else she wanted could be delivered.

Still, she realised that it wasn't a good thing for her to always be cooped up in the house alone. That was when she'd finally decided to hire an in-home carer. Someone who could help her around the house and make sure she took her medication, give some form of social interaction and a much-needed hand in the kitchen. Emily hadn't come highly recommended. In fact, most of the people in her life told her she was crazy to give someone like Emily a chance. Her resume was nonexistent.

Emily had grown up in Sunshine, just as Joanna had, on Bribie Island's eastern shore. But for some reason, none of them knew much about her. And she seemed to mostly keep to herself. Still, Joanna had liked the young woman right off the bat, and so she'd decided not to hire someone with in-home care experience but instead go for the unknown, which had been a risky move at the time but had paid off in spades. Emily had turned out to be the exact right person for the job. The two of them got along well, Emily was a hard worker, and Joanna couldn't be more pleased with the choice she'd made.

Emily was twenty-three years old, which was exactly the kind of youthful antidote to aging that Joanna wanted. At sixty, she had slowed down a little. But she didn't want to give up just yet, even if she struggled more and more to get away from the four walls of her home. And she liked to think that Emily's exuberance for life and positivity kept her young at heart and gave her hope that she could someday do something like take a walk on the open beach again.

At least, Emily always told her she'd do it. "Someday," she'd say. "You're gonna walk down that beach. You'll feel the wind in your hair, the open sky above you, and you'll be happy. I promise."

Joanna clung to those words, even as they scared her. But the fact that Emily believed her promise gave Joanna the strength to believe it as well.

Emily slid a piece of pulled pork into her mouth as she waited for the next tortilla to fry. "Mmmm... It's delicious. Will you include this recipe in your next cookbook?"

"Maybe." Joanna had worked as a head chef at the restaurant she and her husband ran for twenty years, with a break to have children. Now she wrote cookbooks for a living. When Roy died, she'd done her best to keep their dream alive. The long hours and late nights had never really suited her, but she'd made it work. With Ron gone, she struggled to maintain the schedule, the paperwork and to keep the restaurant afloat. Now, she didn't like driving past the place where it'd stood all those years ago. A sad reminder of what once was, the life they'd had, the family they'd grown, the business they'd built together.

They'd spent so many happy times in that restaurant. She hadn't worked full time while raising the children, but she'd still spent many hours a week there. She managed the menu and oversaw the kitchen staff. The children would run and play, hide-and-seek or tag, much to the dismay of the new head chef and the delight of the rest of the staff. They knew every nook and cranny of that place.

She often had to go searching through cupboards and crawl spaces to find them and bring them home at the end of the evening. She'd watched them sit up at the bench to do homework throughout their high school years and even seen them bring dates to eat there once they'd graduated. The restaurant was a big part of their lives, and it saddened her that it was gone. If only one of the kids had wanted to go into the business. But they hadn't. In the end, it wouldn't have made much difference.

Karen had become a teacher and married a school principal down in Melbourne. They only came home for holidays, and their children were now grown too and living all over the world. Brett was a carpenter, and he'd moved to the Sunshine Coast. He was only an hour away, but it might as well have been ten hours. He rarely visited, since his building company kept him busy. And his kids were in high school, which meant they no longer wanted to see her much. They were too occupied with their friends and extracurricular activities.

"Oh, there's the postie. I'm just going to run out and grab the mail," Joanna said suddenly as she spotted him zooming by the front window on his motorbike.

Rain sprinkled across the green grass in her front yard. The sky overhead was grey. But the world was washed clean and bright. There was no point in bringing an umbrella. It was hardly raining. She'd hurry, and then she could dodge most of the drops.

She glanced down at her slippered feet. That wouldn't do. She took them off and slid her feet into the gumboots by the front door. Much better.

Then she took off at a brisk pace in the direction of the

mailbox. Best not to think about it too much. The clouds overhead helped to make the sky seem less big, and she wasn't far from the comfort of the roof over her head. The overhang almost reached her. But still, she was outdoors, and the familiar rush of anxiety washed over her. It elevated her heart rate and made her breathing shallow. Her head felt light, and she squeezed her hands into fists as she pushed herself forwards.

"It's not very far. And I'm fine," she chanted to herself in a bright tone. "What's the worst that could happen?" Probably not the best approach at self-encouragement, but it generally worked well enough.

She spied her neighbour, Chris Hampton, trimming a hanging vine that had climbed over her side of the fence. He glanced up at her with a smile and a wave.

"Good morning, JoJo." He sometimes called her that. It made her feel young. But good grief, the man was obsessed with gardening. Here he was pruning a vine with rain falling down on his wide-brimmed hat.

She waved back, but as she did, her gumboots slid out from underneath her and she flew up into the air and landed on her rear end with a grunt.

The wind was knocked out of her for a moment. She sat up and blinked. "I hope I didn't break anything. Ouch!" She felt along her arms, then both legs. Everything seemed fine. She tried to get back onto her feet, but the panic was weaving its way up her spine. She was stuck out in the open and couldn't get traction with her gumboots on the wet pavement.

Chris was by her side. "Did you hurt yourself? Here, let me help you." He held her by one elbow, and she pressed her weight against him to rise to her feet.

"It's slippery, and I wasn't paying attention," she said as she balanced herself.

"It can happen," he replied. "Are you sure you're okay?"

She patted her rear end. "I think so. Nothing hurts too badly, other than my pride. I'll have some bruising, but I don't think anything's broken."

His kind blue eyes crinkled around the edges. They were the same blue eyes she'd looked into over forty years earlier when the two of them attended the Sunshine State High School together. So much had changed since then. But not his eyes.

"Well, let's get you inside, then," he said.

"I came for the mail," she replied. "And now we're both soaked."

He laughed. "I was soaked before this. And since I'm not made of sugar, I don't think there's any great risk of me dissolving."

He left her standing there and fetched the mail from her mailbox. He tucked it under his arm to keep dry, then took her by the elbow and helped her back to the house. By now, she'd forgotten all about the anxiety. It had flapped away the moment Chris arrived to help.

Chris opened her front door, then removed his own boots and helped her out of hers. Her body was already stiffening. She could tell she'd be struggling with pain throughout their potluck brunch today. Never mind—she'd been through worse.

"What happened?" Emily asked in alarm when she saw them.

"I fell. It's nothing. I'll be fine," Joanna said.

Emily hurried to her side and immediately got to work towelling her dry, finding her a seat and putting her feet up.

Chris watched with an amused expression. "You're well taken care of here."

Joanna smiled as she opened a large manilla envelope. "You have no idea. Emily is truly a godsend. Now, what is this?"

Emily handed Joanna her reading glasses, and she pushed them up the bridge of her nose. "Oh, yes, it's from my publisher. They want to buy the idea we sent them!" She beamed at Emily. "They want to publish *The Sunshine Potluck Society Cookbook*!"

Chapter Two

Debbie Holmes had been practicing law for thirty-eight years, and she wondered if she'd ever grow tired of it. She loved being a barrister. Loved going to bat for her clients. The excitement of it never failed to get her adrenaline pumping. But now she was sixty years old, her husband, Caleb, had asked her to slow down.

"Don't you ever think about retiring?" he'd said to her the previous week.

She'd wanted to reply with something snarky like, "Don't you?" Because the truth was, he worked as many hours as she did, and he hadn't mentioned one thing about retiring yet. But maybe he was thinking about it more than he'd let on. After all, why would he ask her to retire if he didn't intend to do that himself?

She'd always thought they would both retire at sixty-five and travel the world, lounge around tropical swimming pools, and visit all of the cathedrals and museums they'd never had time for in the past. But now that time had almost come, she found she wasn't quite ready for it. She still felt young. The thought of hanging up her barrister's robe terrified her. What would she do with her days? She wasn't the type of woman who'd fostered a series of hobbies or who liked to do charity work. She didn't have a garden; they lived in a high-rise apartment in the city. She couldn't imagine how empty a day would be without work in it.

Still, she couldn't work forever. Could she?

The phone rang, and she answered it as her heels clacked along the tarmac on the way to her car. "Yes, this is Debbie."

"Hi, Deb. It's Evelyne. I need those reports signed by the end of the day." Debbie's firm was a small one. Boutique was the term she preferred. And as the senior partner, she had a very competent assistant. Evelyne was reliable, focused, detail-oriented and had become indispensable in Debbie's life. And because of that, she'd stepped into more of a management role than assistant, really. Debbie had increased her paycheque to reflect that.

"Of course, I forgot. I'll have to do it on my phone because I'm going to be late for the potluck brunch with my friends in Sunshine if I go back up to the apartment now."

"That's fine—you can sign digitally. Also, you have a client appointment at nine am Monday, so don't forget to bring what you need with you. It's right after the partner's meeting."

"I won't forget," Debbie assured her. "Is this for the Herberton lawsuit?"

"That's right. They don't want to settle. Otherwise, I would've set up a mediation. But apparently they want to go to court. It's going to be huge."

"Can you forward me the documents so I can read up on the case before the meeting?" Debbie asked as she unlocked her red sports car.

"Will do," Evelyne replied. "Also, you didn't hear it from me, but Phil is on a rampage again about the dishwasher."

Debbie sighed. "What now?"

"He put up a sign in the office kitchen calling anyone who doesn't put their coffee cup in the dishwasher a *slacker*."

Debbie stifled a laugh. "Okay, I'll deal with it when I'm in the office on Monday."

"It all falls apart when you're not here," Evelyne replied in a singsong voice. "We need you."

Debbie rolled her eyes. She couldn't be out of the office for more than a day or two before the political argy-bargy between the partners began. It was always someone pushing their weight around, attempting to assert their dominance. She wasn't sure what would happen when she finally retired. Phil was the next in charge. He had the most seniority in the partnership besides Debbie, but she couldn't imagine how the rest of the team would survive his tyrannical leadership.

"I know you do. I'll be back on Monday. I've only been gone for three days."

"And it feels like three weeks. See you then!"

She hung up the phone and started the car engine. Three days at a conference in Sydney, and the office was coming apart at the seams. She'd hoped to pull back to a part-time position rather than retire entirely, but if she did that, how would they manage? Would Phil and the other partners collapse in an all-out brawl? And what would the clients think? She'd spent twenty-five years building this firm into a top-notch corporate law firm. Businesses throughout Australia relied on her and her team to manage their legal affairs in court. The last thing she wanted was for her reputation to be ruined by a premature retirement. Especially one she wasn't sure she wanted.

But then there was the issue of Caleb and the fact that they barely talked anymore. They'd been so passionately in love in the early years. But these days, she felt almost as though she didn't know him. Who was he? Who was this man she'd spent the vast majority of her life with? They shared an apartment and a bathroom, even a bed, but they hardly exchanged words more than twice a week. And when they did, it was more like a business discussion than a conversation between lovers.

Was that normal? She was sixty, but she still wanted more from her romantic relationship than that. Did other couples go through the same thing? She hadn't been game to ask her friends. She liked them to think she and Caleb were still as hot and heavy as ever. After all, they'd sacrificed so much for the life they'd built.

Debbie drove through the city and jumped onto the highway. She stopped at a nearby bakery and bought a package of twelve vanilla slices. It wasn't exactly Mexican fare, but she wasn't sure what Mexican desserts looked like, and she was certain she wouldn't find any in a Brisbane café. Besides, the Potluck girls all knew she didn't cook. They wouldn't expect her to bring anything other than her regular café purchase and her camera.

Speaking of the potluck brunch, would Caleb come? She had asked him the previous evening, and he'd grunted something indecipherable in response while he watched the latest cricket match on their enormous flatscreen television set. She couldn't be sure if it was a yes, no or maybe. And she hadn't wanted to push him. He hated when she pushed him.

He hadn't attended one of the brunches in months, but she knew for a fact he didn't have anything on today. He'd gone golfing first thing, but surely he'd be done with nine holes in time to drive to Sunshine. He might be late, but that wouldn't matter. She flicked on the Bluetooth in her car and dialled his number. It went to voicemail, and she left him a message reminding him. She didn't much like the chances of him coming, but it was worth a try.

For a moment, her heart ached. The thought that this was how their marriage would be from now on scared her. She had to do something to pull them out of this free fall, if it wasn't too late already.

Chapter Three

By the time Debbie reached Joanna's house on Bribie Island, the rain had stopped. The sun peeked out from behind a cloud at the newly washed neighbourhood across the road from Sunshine Beach. The house squatted low and quaint behind a white picket fence. The green grass was perfectly clipped beside a garden bed filled with vibrantly coloured flowers.

Debbie climbed out of her car and glanced in the side mirror. She used her hands to smooth down her sleek grey bob. Then she pulled her skirt into place until it reached below her knees. She quickly drew a dash of red lipstick across her lips, then rubbed them together with a smack. She carried her camera bag slung over one shoulder and the baked goods balanced on her palms as she walked carefully down the wet driveway in her heels.

At the door, she knocked then pushed it open. She slipped out of her heels and left them beside the door, then padded into the kitchen in her stockinged feet.

"I'm here! Hello!"

The kitchen smelled of delicious food, spices and marinated meats. But it was otherwise empty. She made her way into the dining room and smiled at the vibrant decor. Gwen always decorated for their themed weeks even though the potluck was held at Joanna's. This time, she'd covered the room in bright colours—orange, pink, blue, green and yellow. There was a straw hat in the centre of the table, along with some beautifully coloured flowers in vases on either side. Each chair had a striped blanket hung over the back, and there was a piñata strung up in one corner of the room.

Debbie laughed. "Gwen, you've had fun this week. It looks great."

Gwen was busy straightening the table runner. "Hey! You made it. Debbie's here!"

Debbie kissed Gwen on the cheek. "Where's Joanna?"

"She and Emily are in her room cleaning up. She had a mishap earlier—took a fall in the driveway."

"Oh, no! Is she okay?"

"I think so. A little bruised. But she said she has something she wants to tell us."

"Colour me intrigued," Debbie replied.

She took her camera out of the bag and got to work taking snapshots around the dining room while they waited for Joanna and Emily to finish up. It was nonsense, really. There was no point in taking so many photographs other than as keepsakes for the four of them. But she liked to keep busy, and she loved photography. Outside of her work, it was her only real passion. She sighed—especially now that Caleb had lost interest in spending time with her.

She checked her phone. He still hadn't called. Surely he'd have finished his round of golf by now.

Joanna hobbled into the room with a walking stick in one hand. "Debbie! How lovely." She kissed her friend on the cheek.

Debbie held her at arm's length to look her over. "Are you hurt? Should we go to the hospital?"

Joanna brushed her off. "I'm fine. I'm only two months older than you. You can't treat me like an old woman yet." She laughed. "But thank you. I appreciate it anyway."

Debbie shook her head. "We're never getting old. Right?"

"Never!...young at heart," Joanna replied.

"Can I get you a drink, Debbie?" Emily asked.

Debbie embraced the young woman. "That would be lovely, honey. How are you this week? Is that nasty cold gone?"

Emily's nose wrinkled. "Mostly. I have a little cough, but nothing much. The eucalyptus oil on my hankie helped, so thanks for that."

"You're welcome. It does the trick every time."

They all returned to the kitchen, where they pulled the meal together. There were burritos and tacos to be eaten with rice and salad. The street corn, or corn off the cob, looked delicious as Debbie followed Joanna's instructions to coat it in butter, mayo, cheese, scallions and salt and pepper. Her mouth watered as she carried the bowl to the table and set it beside a massive pitcher of frozen margaritas.

As they sat around the table, Debbie was overwhelmed by the sudden urge to cry with delight. These friends had been her companions for as long as she could remember. They'd started kindergarten together so many years ago. Their mothers had been friends and had taken them to parks, beaches and swimming pools for play dates. Then they'd done all their schooling together. They'd each gone their own way after university, but they'd come back together when Joanna and Gwen had children.

Debbie and Caleb had never managed to have a family— they'd been too busy with their careers in their twenties and early thirties. By the time they tried to fall pregnant, Debbie

17

found it difficult to conceive, and even when she did, she lost the baby. These ladies were the only family she had left, besides her ever more distant husband.

"I'm so grateful for all of you," was all she said.

She reached out her hands, and Joanna took one, Gwen the other, and squeezed. Emily sat opposite, and she held hands with the women on either side. They bowed their heads to say grace, and then the party began.

Debbie piled her plate high with corn, tortillas, pulled pork, rice and beans, and salad. She always ate a lot at these gatherings. She'd diet tomorrow.

"So, how are things going at the best law firm in the city?" Joanna asked her.

Debbie chewed a mouthful of rice and swallowed. "It's okay, I guess. You'll never imagine what Caleb asked me to do."

Gwen arched an eyebrow. "Do tell."

"He wants me to consider retiring."

The ladies all cried out in astonishment.

Debbie laughed. "Can you picture me in retirement?"

"Not for a moment," Joanna replied. "You'd drive us all crazy and have us organised into committees before we could turn around."

"We'd be fundraising and writing and goodness knows what else. I'd be exhausted, I know that," Gwen added.

"It might not be the worst idea," Emily piped up as she held a glass to her lips. She took a sip. "You could slow down, finally use that beautiful beach house you bought down the street. Have some time to relax..."

"Now, there's an idea," Debbie replied, reaching for her own margarita. "Relax... What is that?"

They all laughed.

"Come on, Deb. You could spend more time with us," Joanna said.

"And you could help me watch the grandkids," Gwen added with a grimace.

"Heavens!" Debbie joked. "How's that going, by the way?"

Gwen sighed. "You all know how much I love my family. My grandchildren are the light of my life. But lately, it seems as though I've become the family babysitting service. I know I did it to myself. I had four children and I spoiled them rotten, and now I must pay!"

Debbie chuckled. "Oh, come on. It can't be that bad."

"I don't like to complain," Gwen continued. "But one of them leaves their children with me most days of the week. They barely even ask anymore—just call to say they're dropping them off because someone is sick and they can't go to daycare or school, or they've got a meeting to attend, or they need some space... Whatever the reason, I've become the person they rely on. And I love that they need me. It's nice to be needed. But it would also be nice to be appreciated."

"I'm sorry, honey," Joanna said, squeezing her hand. "That's hard. I never see my grandchildren, so I can't relate. They're all so busy with their own lives. I wish they'd visit occasionally."

"That's why I shouldn't complain," Gwen replied. "It's a good problem to have, I guess. I'm certainly never lonely. And I can't take that for granted."

There was a knock at the front door. Joanna looked up in surprise. "Now, who could that be?"

Debbie jumped up. "Stay right there, Jo. I'll get it. You need rest."

"Yes. I can't believe you threw all this together when you're injured," Gwen said.

Debbie bustled to the front door and flung it open, expecting to see Caleb on the other side. She was ready to be forgiving that he was late and pile his plate high with good food. The other ladies hadn't seen him in months, and she knew they liked him. Everyone liked him. He was fun to be around, charming and with a witty sense of humour. But lately he'd been so quiet and glum. She hoped it was only a phase.

When she saw who was behind the door, she frowned. It wasn't Caleb. It was a young man who looked to be in his mid-twenties. He was dressed in Army camouflage and had a duffle bag over one shoulder. His cap was pulled low over sparkling green eyes, and there was a dimple in one cheek when he smiled.

"Hey, Deb. How's things?"

She studied his face. Did she know him?

He shifted his stance. "This bag is getting heavy. Do you mind if I come in?"

She frowned. "Aaron?"

He laughed. "Don't tell me you've forgotten me already."

She grinned and threw her arms around his neck. "I can't believe you're here. Jo is going to be so excited to see you. Come on in, soldier. What a surprise!"

Chapter Four

Emily Miller was refilling the pitcher of margaritas from a blender she'd set on the servery when she heard a man's voice in the next room. It was probably Caleb. Debbie always invited her husband to attend their monthly potluck, as did Gwen. But neither man generally came. She couldn't blame them; it was a monthly gabfest of four women, and the two men often found themselves tucked away in the den watching sports instead of at the table. Although the food was worth coming for, in her opinion. And it wasn't big-headed to say so, even though she'd had a hand in most of it, because it was Joanna's skill and expertise that got them here — she was the obedient assistant. Nothing more than that. She'd learned a lot since she first took on the job.

She set the heavy pitcher on the table and glanced through the doorway. The man wore camouflage. That couldn't be Caleb. He always dressed in a dapper style, with impeccable taste but never in military gear.

"Who is that?" she asked.

Joanna looked up and let out a cry. She pushed herself to

her feet and fumbled for the walking cane. "Oh, blast. Can you please help me, Emily?"

Emily gave Joanna the cane before she rushed out into the kitchen. She launched herself at the man, who laughed as he caught her.

"Aaron!" she cried as she cupped his cheeks between her hands and gazed up at his face.

He leaned down to kiss her forehead. "Hey, Granny. I thought I'd surprise you."

"And you most definitely did."

"What's with the cane?" he asked, concern etched on his face.

"I fell earlier, but I'm fine. Come in and take a seat. We're eating, and there's plenty to go around. I hope you're hungry."

"I'm starved, but do you mind if I take a shower and change first? It's been a long trip."

Emily took a step back and hid behind the wall of the dining room. Gwen joined the other ladies in greeting Aaron, but Emily clutched her hands to her chest, heart thumping. Aaron was back in Sunshine. She'd had the biggest crush on him in high school. And yes, it was eight years since he'd graduated and joined the Army. He'd broken her heart when he left. But even though so much time had passed, it seemed like yesterday.

The familiar jolt of adrenaline, the sweating palms, the racing heart. She remembered it all. He'd been the best friend of her older brother, Tristan. The two of them had been inseparable. Aaron had spent most of his spare time at their house, swimming in the pool with them or playing table tennis. Watching movies or eating meals together.

He'd been the cutest guy in school, and she'd loved him from a distance for two heartbreaking years. Now he was back on the island and visiting Joanna, his grandmother. How long would he be there? Probably not long. Maybe he was on furlough. She hadn't seen him since he graduated, but she always knew it was a possibility he would show up on Joanna's doorstep. She'd mistakenly believed she'd have warning and could've made an excuse to be out when the time came.

He didn't come into the dining room, and soon she heard the sound of the shower turning on. Her shower. In the guest bathroom, true, but it was the bathroom she used. All her things were in there. Her loofah, her pink tube of face wash, her razor. She pressed her hands to her cheeks. There was no polite way to get out of there. She'd have to face him when he was done in the shower. But how would she play it? Was she still annoyed with him? He'd left without a word. But then, he didn't owe her anything. He'd stolen her first kiss, but that was an entirely different story that she didn't have time to obsess about now. He probably didn't even remember. He'd acted as though it didn't happen.

The ladies returned to the dining room, chatting happily about how exciting it was to have Joanna's grandson back after all this time.

"Were you expecting him?" Debbie asked as they sat again.

Joanna was beaming. "No, I had no idea. He could've called. But it's very like him. He's the impulsive one."

"You were just saying how none of them visits, and now look," Gwen said with a teary smile. "It's wonderful."

"Don't get me started." Joanna sniffled as she patted her cheeks with a cloth napkin. "I'll run my makeup."

"What's he doing here? Visiting or staying?" Emily asked as she topped up everyone's drinks.

Joanna shrugged. "I don't know. We haven't got around to talking about that yet. I'm sure he's tired and hungry. He's come right from Darwin. It's not far on the plane, but apparently he had a long truck ride before that. And he hasn't showered or eaten in two days. We'll have to get some food into him before we bombard him with questions."

* * *

By the time Aaron was showered and dressed, the ladies had finished their main course and were chatting over another glass of margaritas. He peeped through the doorway.

"Should I get a plate?"

Gwen hurried to help him. "I'll get you one, sweetheart. You take a seat at the table. You must be exhausted. And your granny isn't feeling her best."

Aaron sat in the only empty chair, beside Emily. She did her best to smile and not let her jackhammering heart betray her. He looked better than in high school. He'd filled out in a good way. His hair was shorter, but still thick and dark, wet from the shower. His face had matured, and he had an even more athletic build than he had before. He wore a pair of board shorts and a T-shirt.

"Hi," he said. "I'm Aaron."

He didn't recognise her. How was that possible? Surely she hadn't changed so much. Although she'd only been fifteen when he left. So, she could probably cut him a break.

"I know," she replied. "I'm Emily."

"Oh, do we know each other?"

"Emily Miller... Tristan's sister."

Recognition flashed across his handsome face. "Oh, little Emily-Bug."

Her cheeks flushed with warmth. "Yes, well, I don't really go by that name anymore."

He laughed. "Of course, sorry. Good to see you again, Emily. I wasn't expecting you to be here." He glanced up at his grandmother, confusion on his face. No doubt he was wondering how Emily fit into the Sunshine Potluck Society his granny held every month with her sixty-year-old friends.

"Emily works as my in-home carer, darling," Joanna said. "I'm sure I told you that. She helps take care of me and with the cookbooks."

"Cool. Maybe you told me. Sorry, I forgot."

Great, she was unrecognisable and forgettable. A perfect combination.

"And sorry for not recognising you," he whispered with a wink. "You've really grown up."

She wasn't about to be taken in again by the former bad boy of Sunshine High. She'd already gone down that path once, and she wasn't about to fall for him again. It would only mean another broken heart.

Chapter Five

Debbie Holmes liked to sit and listen to the conversation going on around her. It wasn't that she was quiet. She was a chatterbox most of the time. But when she was with her Potluck Society friends, she could enjoy taking in their banter while she ate. It gave her time to reflect. And there were things on her mind. Things she needed to think through. After their meal, Emily had left the table to go to her room, and Aaron was in the den watching TV. It was only the three of them, and she relished these moments.

"You're deep in thought," Joanna said.

"Am I?" Debbie asked.

Gwen smiled. "I'm usually the quiet one."

Joanna nodded. "You're right, although I miss you when you're not around, Gwen. I had to watch the finals of *Australian Idol* without you. It wasn't the same. Emily was out for dinner with her family, so I was here all alone. It's fun to cheer for people when you're with friends, but it's just plain kooky to do it when you're in an empty house."

"Who won?" Debbie asked.

"It was that girl with all the curls. I can't remember her name."

"Oh, good," Gwen added. "I wanted her to win. Sorry I couldn't be here. I've been so busy lately."

"Completely understandable."

Joanna didn't get out of the house much. Ever since the incident with the restaurant, she'd become more and more of a recluse. Gwen worried about her. She needed to try to get Joanna to venture out more often, or one day she'd simply stop trying. She could see it happening in front of her eyes but wasn't sure what to do about it.

"How are things with Caleb?" Gwen asked Debbie. "It's a shame he couldn't make it today. Please tell him hello from me."

Debbie set her cocktail back on the table and leaned forward. "I'll tell him, thanks. But I don't know that he'll hear me."

"What do you mean?" Joanna asked.

Debbie smoothed her glossy grey bob with one hand. "He doesn't seem to listen these days. Every time I speak to him, all I get in response is a grunt or nothing at all. He's so focused on his phone or the television. He works all the time. I feel like we're drifting apart, but the more I try to get his attention and pull us back together, the worse it becomes. It's like being a teenager the popular boy doesn't notice all over again. I never thought I'd be back here."

In high school, Debbie had been tall and skinny with knobby knees. She hadn't gotten much attention from boys. But as soon as she graduated college, things had changed. She dressed in glamorous outfits and got her hair done at the salon. She had her nails painted and always wore perfectly applied makeup. And she'd managed to attract the attention of the very dapper and extremely successful Caleb Holmes. Caleb came from a wealthy family and was a barrister, like Debbie.

When she'd started her own small firm, he'd taken on a role as partner in his family's prestigious corporate law firm. They'd both prioritised their careers, and both had done very well.

They'd fallen in love hard and fast when she was twenty-seven and he was twenty-nine years old. His family had approved of the match. Her family loved him like a son. It was the perfect relationship. They enjoyed the same things, skiing and rock climbing, photography and playing the stock market. And neither one of them had much of an interest in children. They seemed like the perfect match.

But then it turned out that they never had time for skiing or rock climbing. Even though Debbie still loved photography, Caleb had lost interest. And instead of spending time together, he'd taken up golf, something Debbie hated. She was far too uncoordinated to hit straight down the green, and they always ended up in a terrible mood when she played.

"Is that normal?" Debbie asked. "Do you think it's how marriage goes? Are my expectations too high?"

"I think it can be normal," Gwen replied.

"But it doesn't have to be," Joanna said. "Ron and I were always close. But we worked hard at it. It doesn't happen without some effort. We had to choose to spend time together and love each other every day."

"I don't know what to do," Debbie said, feeling even more hopeless. "I've tried to get his attention—I've suggested outings together. I sent him an article about regular date nights. I've invited him to this brunch every month. But nothing seems to help."

"It's hard to keep the intimacy going in a marriage. Especially when you're busy. You've got the business; he has his family's firm. There's a lot going on," Gwen said in a soothing tone. "Don't be too hard on each other."

"I'm trying not to be. But I'm worried," Debbie replied. "What if he doesn't want to fix this gap between us? Is this it?

This is how my life and my marriage will be from now on?" The thought made her throat tight.

"I wish I had the answer," Gwen replied with a frown. "I don't know how to get Duncan's attention either. And he always takes me for granted. I'm sure I've done it to myself. I've tried so hard to be the perfect homemaker and mother, that it's all the family expects of me. I have to discover Duncan's stinky gym clothes in his bag, since he never actually puts them in the hamper. Usually they're in the back of his car or shoved under the side of the bed."

"Really?" Joanna asked and rolled her eyes.

Gwen sighed. "Yesterday, I went looking for them and found the bag. It had his business shirt and pants in it, instead of the usual dirty workout gear, which was strange. He generally showers and changes at the gym. So, I sniffed them to see if they were dirty—maybe he'd forgotten to take his regular gym clothes. They smelled like a perfume of some kind, but not one I own." She paused and looked up, her eyes red-rimmed. "That's bad, isn't it?"

Debbie's heart ached for her friend. "It might be nothing, honey. Don't read too much into it."

"She's right," Joanna agreed. "Give him a chance to explain. Maybe they were handing out samples at the mall. Or perhaps he hugged a coworker."

"I guess you're right. I shouldn't jump to conclusions," Gwen replied.

But the atmosphere had changed. They were all thinking it. Was Duncan having an affair? After all these years together, decades of her raising their four children, now caring for their grandchildren, helping build his business and their dream home. Would he do that to Gwen?

Chapter Six

After dessert, the group moved to the sunroom at the back of the house by the swimming pool for coffee. Joanna was feeling sore but had taken some pain relief earlier, and it seemed to be helping. She was pleased with how the brunch had gone.

Gwen had brought decorations and homemade churros with chocolate sauce. As usual, Debbie had photographed everything and brought a package of baked goodies from her local bakery. And the entire thing had been topped off with the arrival of her favourite grandson (she knew she shouldn't have a favourite but couldn't help herself).

Aaron had gone for a nap. He said he hadn't been sleeping well lately. She was grateful that she always kept the guest room made up in case of visitors. He was napping while she and her friends enjoyed the air-conditioning and looked out over her thriving garden and sparkling pool. They'd had plenty of rain lately, and she loved to get out in the garden and work on her flower beds. It was hard to ignore the anxiety that open spaces sometimes gave her, but she felt it was important for her to do what she could to challenge herself in that area.

"I wanted to talk to you ladies about something," she said.

Emily joined them and was filling a cup with tea from a floral teapot. She smiled and gave a nod to Joanna. She was as excited as Joanna was about their pet project.

"What is it?" Debbie asked.

"I didn't tell you, but I submitted an idea to my publisher. I pitched a cookbook about our monthly brunch called *The Sunshine Potluck Society Cookbook*. And they want to buy it!"

Debbie laughed with delight and clapped her hands together.

Gwen blinked. "Really? They're going to publish a book about us?"

"That's right," Joanna replied. "The book will include all our recipes from our themed potlucks. And will feature photographs of our gatherings. Your decor, Gwen, and your photography, Debbie. They said we could include written commentary by all of us. Anecdotes, stories, whatever we like."

"Isn't it amazing?" Emily asked.

Gwen hurried to embrace Joanna, and then Emily, then Debbie. Soon they were all laughing and hugging.

"I can't believe it," Debbie said. "I've never published a book before."

"Me neither," Gwen said.

"Same," Emily added. "It's old hat for Jo, but not for the rest of us."

"I still get a thrill every time," Joanna replied. "And this time, I get to share it with all of my friends, so I'm even more excited than usual. Besides, I think the book will look spectacular. And the concept is really interesting. My editor loved it."

"When will all this happen?" Debbie asked as she resumed her seat.

"We need to finalise the content by the end of March, and then it will be done with editing in July and released in November. So, it'll be nine months from now before we see it in print."

"Wow, it takes a while. Kind of like growing a baby," Gwen replied.

"Yes! That's the publishing process. And in fact, that's actually quite quick," Joanna said. "I'm sure the time will fly. And we've got a lot to get done by the end of the month. It will keep us busy."

"You're right," Emily said, suddenly looking anxious. "How will we get it all done?"

"We'll work together," Debbie said with a quick nod of her head. "We're intelligent, capable women. I'm sure we can manage."

Chapter Seven

Emily slipped a pair of headphones on, tied her hair into a ponytail and got to work cleaning up. The monthly brunch was over. Gwen and Debbie had gone home. Joanna was resting. She looked exhausted after all that cooking, and there was a gigantic bruise down the back of her thighs where she'd fallen.

Emily had given Joanna some more medicine then helped her into bed. Now she was working on cleaning up the mess they'd made. The kitchen looked as though a bomb had gone off. There were bowls and pans stacked up in the sink and dirty dishes piled around it. The ladies had helped wash the initial load of dishes and put away the remnants of the meal that'd been brought out of the dining room before they left. But there was still a lot to be done.

They'd sealed the leftovers into small containers and found room for them in the refrigerator. Gwen and Debbie had taken some home. The rest would be perfect for lunches over the next few days. Especially since she had to go out tomorrow. Her sister was going through chemotherapy, and Emily liked to visit and help out around the house. Especially since

Wanda had two small children and got tired easily with her treatments.

Brian, her boyfriend, was gone. Their mother had moved to northern QLD as soon as Emily graduated, so it was mostly left to Emily to support Wanda. And even though it was hard, she liked taking care of people. It was why she'd gravitated towards the job with Joanna. Something about looking after and nurturing others gave her joy. She was exhausted at the end of a long day, but she felt good about what she'd achieved. And when she had to clean up, like today, she could put on her headphones, pump up the music and revel in the satisfaction of cleaning surfaces, plumping cushions and tidying rooms.

The one person she couldn't stop thinking about was Aaron. What would it be like to live with a man? She'd never done it. She'd lived with her brother, Tristan, until he was eighteen, when he'd moved out to attend university. But she'd never lived with a *man*. Her father had left when she was five years old; she barely remembered him being in the house with them.

Now Aaron had moved in. For how long? She didn't know. She'd overheard he and Joanna talking about him staying until he got on his feet. But how long did something like that take? It seemed he'd left the military—honourable discharge, he'd said. So, what would he do now?

He was in the room next to hers. She wasn't sure how she felt about that. Surely it would be fine. No doubt he'd get a job and she'd hardly see him. Still, it felt strange to know he was there, behind his bedroom door. After all this time, he was a stranger to her and yet also felt familiar. She glanced at the doorway and imagined him in there. Then she shook her head and hurried to find the vacuum cleaner in the hall closet.

With the vacuum running, she had to amp up the volume of the music so she could hear it. She preferred upbeat songs.

Something that would help give her the energy she needed to get through the afternoon's work. She bopped and swayed as one of her favourites came on. Then she shut her eyes and held up the end of the vacuum like a microphone. She was a famous singer on stage, and the crowd was going wild as she reached for the high note.

What if Aaron expected her to be his carer as well? She took care of Joanna, but would he want the same treatment? He was a grown man. Surely he wouldn't need that. But maybe Joanna would want her to cook for him, do his laundry, clean up after him the same way she did for Joanna. It would be strange, although it wouldn't add a lot to her workload. Her job was fairly easy, and she was paid well for it. She didn't mind the extra work. Only, it would be awkward to take care of Aaron, with the history they'd shared.

Not that he seemed to remember any of it.

She sighed and vacuumed up a few corn kernels that someone had dropped on the dining room carpet.

He was sleeping a lot. He'd said he was taking a nap about two hours ago and hadn't come out of his room yet. Would he sleep this much every day?

She should ignore him. He wasn't going to disrupt her life. She wouldn't let him. She had a good life. She loved her job. Joanna was good to her and gave her flexibility to help her sister whenever she needed. She had a group of friends she'd known since high school. She had everything going for her. Aaron Gilston being back in town would make no difference to her whatsoever.

She turned towards the dining table and worked on a stubborn set of corn kernels. Those little things had managed to tumble all over the place. There were some stuck behind the door. She closed the door most of the way to get to them. Then she moved around the door, opening it again and backing out into the hallway.

When she turned around to march towards the kitchen, she ran smack-dab into a strong, wet and very naked chest.

* * *

Emily's cheek was pressed to Aaron's chest. She dropped the vacuum cleaner nozzle and grabbed hold of him with both hands to steady herself. She'd been moving quickly, dancing and hurrying with her headphones blocking out all other sounds. She hadn't noticed him leave the bedroom. He wore a beach towel wrapped around his waist, and somehow his arms had found their way around her.

It felt good. Too good. Her face flushed with warmth, and she took a step back, then wiped the pool water from her cheek.

When she removed her headphones, she heard him laughing quietly. "You okay?"

She nodded. "I'm so sorry. I didn't hear you or see you. I was vacuuming and had the music turned up loud..."

"I can see that." His eyes twinkled. "I thought I'd take a swim. It's such a beautiful day. And I couldn't wake up after my nap. You must think I'm such a grandpa, taking a nap in the middle of the day. But honestly, I haven't had much sleep lately. It's been a rough few months."

"No, it's fine. I like naps myself. Well, not usually because I hate that groggy feeling that you have afterwards, like you're living in a dream world or something. But I like the idea of naps." She was babbling. He made her nervous.

He smiled at her as he wiped the dripping water from his forehead with the end of his towel. It came unravelled and revealed his blue and green board shorts slung low around his toned hips. She quickly looked away. He'd really worked out since the last time she'd seen him in a swimsuit. Like, a lot.

"Hey, I was wondering... Can you tell me where the laundry is in this place? I need to wash a few things."

She busied herself unplugging the vacuum to move it. "Oh, you can put your clothes in the hamper in the laundry room. I usually do a load in the mornings."

He hesitated. "I didn't mean for you to do it. I'm going to wash my clothes. You work for Granny, not for me."

Good to know. "Are you sure? I don't mind."

"That would be way over the line. I don't want to cause any trouble for you or Granny. I don't know how long I'll be here, but I promise not to add to your workload. Besides, I've been taking care of myself for eight years. I don't know how to do it any other way."

She nodded. "Fair enough. The laundry room is through the garage by the pool. The clothesline is behind the garage."

He waved goodbye and headed to his bedroom. Emily watched him go, her heart thudding in her ribcage. At least he'd answered her unspoken question—he didn't expect her to take care of him. That was a relief. No awkward dirty underwear to deal with. Hopefully he'd manage his own dirty dishes and crumbs in his bedroom as well. But even with that conversation taken care of, no matter what she told herself, having him here changed everything. And it was ridiculous for her to pretend otherwise.

Chapter Eight

Debbie set the phone back in its cradle and tidied the tray filled with scattered pieces of paper on the end of her desk. She hated an untidy desk. But lately, things had been so hectic that her office was in complete disarray. She straightened the blotter and her line of pens, along with her laptop and calendar. That was better. She'd have to deal with the stacks of file boxes in the corner later. Or maybe she'd get Evelyne onto them.

"Evelyne," she said over the intercom.

"Yes, Debbie?"

"Do you think you'd have time to take these files back to the file room for me?"

"No problem at all. Also, Phil wants to see you. Should I send him in, or do you want him to make an appointment?"

"Thanks, Ev. You can send him in now."

She was going through her inbox when Phil came into her office and shut the door behind him. He was balding, and his hair was shaved short. He wore a suit and tie, but the tie hung slightly loose and crooked against his white shirt.

"Good morning, Phil. How are you today?"

He sat in the large plush leather chair opposite her dark hardwood timber desk. "I'm doing okay. How about you?"

"Great, thanks."

"How was the conference?"

"I made some contacts. Good chance to network. All in all, I think it was worthwhile. How was the office?"

He shrugged. "No one can remember to put their coffee cups in the dishwasher. But other than that, it was fine."

She hid a smile behind her hand. "I'm sure you'll sort that out in no time."

"We've got a leadership team meeting in ten. I thought I'd update you before that gets started."

"I appreciate that, Phil. You're always so thoughtful."

She did appreciate him. He was an efficient and hard worker. Very focused and dedicated to his job. Sometimes a little too focused. But she also knew him well enough to realise that he had an agenda. He wanted to get her onside over some kind of political situation in the office.

"You know that Stuart and Renee have been working on the Harding case for six months. And now that they're on the home stretch, Greg is trying to horn in on the action and be part of the team when it's clear they're going to win. He wants to argue the case in court, even though they're the ones who've pulled the entire case together."

She steepled her hands together on the desk while she listened. "Okay."

"I told him to stay out of it. But he said he's going to bring it up in the leadership meeting. I know you'll back me up on this."

"Thanks for letting me know. I understand."

He studied her with a wary look. "So, what are you going to say?"

She inhaled a slow breath. "I know they've worked really hard on this case. But we're a team. Greg is a closer. He is the best we've got when it comes to presenting a case in court. They should take advantage of that. If he wins for them, we all win."

Phil's face grew red. "If that's what you think."

"I do," she said. "I'll let Stuart and Renee know. I'm sure the bonuses they'll receive if they win the case will be convincing."

When he left her office, she sat in silence for a while, staring at the closed door. Phil wanted to take over the firm when she retired. He'd told her that about five years earlier. His sights were firmly set on the senior partner position that she'd held for twenty years. And even though he was a very capable barrister, she was still undecided about putting her baby, her firm, into his hands. It was their unspoken agreement. But, she'd worked so hard to build the firm's reputation as a high-class, elegant and well-run team. If he took over, she was concerned about him running it into the ground with his competitiveness and internal spats with the other partners and staff.

It was one of the reasons she was so reluctant to retire. But Caleb had asked her to slow down. And she knew that she needed to do whatever it took to save her marriage. What good would it be if she saved her firm but not her marriage? She couldn't imagine life without Caleb. How could she grow old alone? She'd always pictured the two of them side by side. Was it too late? Was he already out of reach?

She wiped tears from the corners of her eyes, stood and straightened her suit, then strode to the boardroom for the meeting.

The room was already full. There were six partners around the table. It wasn't a large firm, but it was one she was immensely proud of building.

"Good morning, everyone. Thank you so much for being here promptly. And I appreciate all of you pitching in to keep things running last week while I was away at the conference." She sat at the head of the table and laid her hands on the dark timber surface. "It was a very productive time. I have some business cards to give out to each of you for follow-up."

There were nods and murmurs of greeting from around the table. Phil sat at the other end. His brow was furrowed. Evelyne pulled up a chair by the door, her laptop on a small lap desk. She would take the minutes so they could refer to them throughout the week.

"I want to open the meeting with the first order of business." Debbie cleared her throat and pushed her grey bob back behind her ears. "I've wanted to slow down my pace of work for a while now. I know we're very busy and there's a lot going on, but at some stage, we all have to make decisions about what's best for us and our families."

She saw the interest and curiosity drift across Phil's face as he sat up straighter in his chair.

"So, I'll be moving to a three-day work week starting from today. I'll take two days off per week, depending on client appointments and court dates. It's a trial. I'll revisit and reassess in three months. If it hasn't worked for us, I'll come up with a different solution. But I'm confident we can make it work." Her heart hammered in her throat. She wasn't confident at all. She was terrified the firm would sink without her there every single day. As Evelyne had recently told her, it didn't work when she wasn't there. And Debbie knew that was the risk she was taking.

"Two days?" Phil asked. "I'm sure we can manage without you for two days a week."

There were murmurs of agreement, although she noted shock on some faces. She hadn't expected anything else from Phil. He looked downright smug. No doubt he was keen to get her out of the way so he could take charge of more of their top clients. He was the most ruthlessly ambitious man she'd ever met and normally she loved that about him — it made it easy to get him to do things the way she wanted him to. But now she wasn't so sure it would work out in her favour. Still, what else could she do? She relied on him to keep the company going.

"I appreciate all of your support. Let's get to the other items on the agenda..."

Chapter Nine

Gwen lived in a big house on a round hill behind Joanna's street. Bribie Island was a small, mostly flat island off the coast of southeast Queensland. It was joined to the mainland by a long bridge over the Pumicestone Passage.

Sunshine was a cozy hamlet that huddled around a bay on the eastern shoreline. Gwen could see the ocean from her front verandah, and she often sat there with a cup of coffee to mull over things while she watched waves crash against the golden sand. There was something therapeutic about the steady rhythm and the shushing sound. It comforted her.

And today, she needed that. She took a sip of coffee and leaned back in her chair. A magpie warbled in the gumtree in the front yard. She hadn't been able to stop thinking about her husband's shirt and the perfume she'd smelled on it. Debbie thought Gwen should confront him, but she wasn't ready to do that. She hated confrontation on the best of days. But something like this — it might mean the end of her marriage. Would it be better to know or not know? Would it be better to leave things as they were and put up with the uncertainty, or to uncover the truth?

She honestly couldn't say.

It was easy when she was twenty and single to declare that she'd never put up with infidelity and she wanted to know the absolute truth from her future husband. But now she was sixty years old, and she'd spent a lifetime with the man she loved, raising four children with him. When the family gathered for an event, there were ten grandchildren. And it was bedlam. But in a good way.

She loved the noise and chaos of her family get-togethers. But what she didn't like was that her husband, children and grandchildren were all perfectly happy to let her manage everything on her own. She'd clean the house, buy the food, prepare and serve the food, then clean up afterwards. Sometimes her daughter would offer to wash the dishes, but her three sons never lifted a finger. They took after their father that way. And now that they were raising children of their own, they expected her to also help them with that.

At thirty-five, Brandon was the eldest. He had four children with his wife, Mara. They'd been separated for over twelve months, and on the weeks he had the children, he often drove them over to Gwen's and dropped them off so he could run errands, or go on a date, or even go cycling. At first, she'd been happy to do it. He'd always been a lovely boy, so handsome and charming. And he needed her. His marriage was on the rocks, and he was struggling. She could see that. But that was a year ago, and it seemed more and more that he was taking advantage.

Now that they'd reconciled, Gwen was extremely grateful to see him happy again, but he seemed to feel entitled to leave the kids with her, without a word of thanks.

His brothers, Hilton and Frank, had followed his example. They were both married, but they often dropped the children with her without asking first. They assumed she'd be home and have nothing else to do.

"I've got to work, Mum. See you after five," was all they'd say by way of explanation.

She didn't mind. Of course she didn't. She loved that her children saw her as someone they could rely on. It showed that her boys loved her and her parenting style. They were comfortable having her help to raise their children. But she was tired. And there were other things she wanted to do with her life.

She'd been waiting and waiting for Duncan to retire so the two of them could finally spend time together, travel, enjoy the fruits of their labour. And now his shirt, the perfume—it could change everything. Or maybe it was nothing. Maybe she was getting worked up over something silly. There were a dozen possible explanations for the scent. Now that some time had passed, she couldn't recall exactly how it had smelled. She didn't know if it meant anything at all. And she wasn't sure she wanted to.

The doorbell rang. She set her coffee cup down on a small wicker glass-top table and hurried to open it. Brandon stood on her doorstep with the four children. All of them were under the age of ten. It was Monday morning. The two older kids were supposed to be in school. But both had on casual clothes rather than their uniforms, although they did have their backpacks. She knew what this meant. Her day was about to be completely hijacked.

"Hello, my darlings. How are you all?"

"Hey, Mum, not so great. Kimmy and Nolan are sick, and the two younger ones say they have sore throats. I can't take them to daycare. They've really cracked down on people bringing sick kids."

She offered a sympathetic smile. Each of the kids either looked miserable or bored. The younger ones ran at her legs and threw their arms around a knee each.

"Nanna!"

She couldn't help laughing. "You're going to knock me over one of these days. You're getting so big."

"I'll be back to get them around five. Maybe six. Work has been crazy." He waved goodbye and jogged down the front path to his idling SUV.

Gwen ushered the four children inside, then stood in the doorway to watch him drive away. He hadn't said please or thank you. She didn't raise him like that. When had he decided to do away entirely with his manners? Maybe she'd been too slack, always giving in. She'd spoiled him.

With a sigh, she shut the door then walked to the kitchen, where she found the children had all dropped their backpacks and were either rummaging in the fridge or playing with the TV remote.

"How about we all make fresh, hot pikelets for morning tea, and then you can do some painting?" she trilled.

The younger kids were soon absorbed in mixing pikelet batter, but the older kids retreated to the den with their iPads. Gwen helped them to pour large spoonfuls of the batter into her electric frying pan. Then she flipped them over when they bubbled on top.

Before long, the kids had batter on their noses and cheeks from licking out the bowl. When finally the golden pikelets were done, they ate them with lashings of creamy butter and strawberry jam she'd made from her garden in the cool autumn months. Then she cleaned them up and sat them on the closed-in back porch with watercolour paints and easels.

She made sure the outer door was locked, set the baby monitor she'd purchased years ago on the BBQ, and then retreated inside to do some housework. The laundry was still in the dryer from days ago. It'd be wrinkled now, and she'd have to iron it all. But she hadn't been in the mood to finish it up after she'd smelled the perfume. Now that some time had passed, she was ready to get it finished and hung up.

She reached for Duncan's shirt, smoothed it out and studied the collar. Was that lipstick? No, surely not. She was imagining things. It was a small pink smudge. She'd have to wash the shirt again to get that out of the fabric. She held it up to her nose and breathed in deeply. It smelled like a field of daisies now after going through the washer and dryer. Then she tossed it into a bucket of hot water to soak with bleach and finished the rest of the laundry.

When she returned to the back deck, the older kids had hung up everyone's paintings to dry on the line with pegs she'd strung up for that purpose. And she took them inside for lunch and a movie in the den. She sat on the couch with them. One child on her left, snuggled into her side. Another on her right, head on her thigh. The other two sat at her feet, cuddling up to each leg. These were her favourite moments. When everyone was quiet and close. It felt good to be loved.

But it would also be nice to be appreciated. She'd never said anything to Brandon, or the other adults in her family, about it. Maybe it was time. She didn't want much. She was happy to help. In fact, she loved it. She'd dedicated her life to caring for her family. She'd raised her children with very little help. Neither her parents nor Duncan's were nearby. She'd done without babysitters, without the village that people like to talk about. And she'd relished every moment.

She was born to do this. It was her favourite thing in the world — being a mother, a grandmother. Still, she was supposed to be retired by this age, lounging by a pool, pottering in a garden or travelling the world. It would be nice to have a little time to herself now and then. And she could do with a rest, maybe a nap each afternoon. Even without all of that, she would manage with a kind word, the occasional thank you. She was feeling unappreciated. Especially by Duncan. If he was stepping out on her after all of her years of faithfulness, love and care, she simply wouldn't understand.

Chapter Ten

When Emily awoke on Tuesday morning, she vowed to do better. To stop thinking so much about Aaron sleeping in the next room. Instead, she'd focus on her work. She had a job to do, and that job was getting busier now that she and Joanna were putting together the book for her publisher. *The Sunshine Potluck Society Cookbook* had become an all-consuming, time-sucking project that she and Joanna couldn't get enough of. It was intoxicating pulling together the photographs, the recipes, the stories and anecdotes. It was still a hot mess, but she could see the potential. And it excited her.

Joanna had even agreed to list her and all of the members of their monthly brunch group as authors. She would be a published author. As she lay on her back, staring at the ceiling above her bed, a little thrill ran down her spine. An author! She never imagined in her wildest dreams that would happen. It was only a partial credit. It wasn't her book entirely, but her name would be on it. And she loved the idea.

She swung her feet over the edge of the bed and got up with a yawn. Sunlight streamed through the edge of the drapes in a slanted rectangle of light on the hardwood floor. She showered and dressed, then helped Joanna get ready for the day. Joanna didn't need much assistance, but Emily liked to bring her a cup of coffee in bed and then make her bed and plump her pillows while Joanna showered.

Then she got to work cooking breakfast for all three of them. Aaron usually joined them to eat and then headed out to his newly acquired job in the city. He'd bought a new wardrobe, with Emily's help. He'd asked her if she would mind going shopping with him, and she said she'd be happy to help. They'd spent the entire day at a nearby shopping centre on the mainland picking out dress shirts, slacks, belts and shoes.

He'd had a haircut as well, and she'd chosen from the book of photographs which one she liked best. He'd shown it to the hairdresser and came out looking even more dapper than ever. His hair was already short from his time in the military, but now it was sculpted in a fashionable style, and when dressed in his new business attire, he was strikingly handsome.

As she scrambled eggs and fried bacon for their breakfast, she couldn't help remembering him dressed up in a suit for his year twelve formal. He'd worn a black suit with a bow tie. The only one in the entire year to sport a bow tie. He'd stood out from the crowd then, just as he did now. Only back then, he'd been the school's bad boy. The resident rebellious teen. He often did things that made her wonder what he was thinking — like jumping off the bridge into the bay or joyriding in his uncle's boat without his permission. She was the type of girl who always played by the rules, so his carefree attitude made her nervous. All the girls had a crush on him, but he seemed not to notice. He lived his life as though no one was watching, and she'd always admired and been envious of that.

Joanna emerged from her bedroom looking fresh and happy. She was smiling from ear to ear and carrying the folder they were using to store all of their photographs and recipes for the cookbook layout under one arm.

"It's a beautiful day!" she said, setting the folder down on the dining table.

"Yes, it is. Not a cloud in the sky."

"I'm excited to work on our cookbook," Joanna replied as she opened the folder. "I suppose we should wait until after breakfast, although I hate to put it off."

"Yes, let's eat first, and then we can dive in. I've been thinking about the layout for the French theme. We should definitely use some of the pictures you took when you last visited Paris. Don't you think?"

"I'd like to. And I want to share an anecdote about a pastry shop I visited while I was there. The croissants were divine." Joanna closed the folder again, then came to the kitchen to help Emily carry the plates to the table.

Steam rose from the eggs and bacon. Butter melted in small pools on the edges of the toast.

She set the plates on the table, then returned to the kitchen to pour them each a coffee. It was hot and black. The milk and sugar were on the table for people to add as they preferred.

Aaron burst in through the front door. He wore a singlet top with a pair of athletic shorts. His body was bathed in sweat, and he was breathing hard.

"Oh, dear! You're dripping sweat on the floor." Joanna clapped her hands to her cheeks.

"Good morning," he said with a grin. "Sorry, Gran." His teeth were white against his tanned face. He had on a pair of reflective sunglasses which he pushed up on top of his head.

"Good morning," Emily said, suddenly feeling shy. "I made eggs."

"Perfect," he replied. "I'll have a quick shower and join you." He jogged down the hallway.

Emily met Joanna's gaze. Joanna was smiling with a knowing look. "He's a nice boy."

"Yes, he is," Emily said, busying herself with setting the table with glasses of juice.

Joanna watched her a moment, then sat at the table. Emily joined her. They said grace and began to eat. It only took Aaron a few minutes to join them. Now he had wet hair and wore a sea-green T-shirt with the collar turned up.

"How far did you run today?" Emily asked.

"Five kilometres. I have to eat quickly and head to work. We've got a team meeting at nine thirty."

"How's work going?" Joanna asked.

Aaron gulped down a mouthful of juice. "It's good so far. A lot to learn. It's very different to the Army. A lot of meetings and chitchat. I'll get used to it."

"Is your boss nice?" Emily asked.

He met her gaze. His green eyes were dark and intense, and she had to look away. "He's okay so far. He says things like 'alrighty then,' and 'if you have to say it twice, it wasn't worth saying once.' But he's fine. I'm learning a lot from him. It's a good job. I just wish I could stay on the island. I love it here. It's such a relief after all the deserts and tropical ovens I've been living in the past few years. There's a breeze, the ocean is perfect, you can swim in it without worrying about crocs or jellyfish, and bonus, I get to live in a great house with two beautiful women." He winked, and Emily felt herself blush against her will.

Joanna laughed. "Get away with you, boy. You've always been a charmer."

He laughed too. "You know me, Gran. I can't help myself. So, what are you two up to today?"

"We're working on our cookbook," Joanna replied.

He took a bite of eggs. "How's it going?"

"It's coming together," Emily said. "We're doing themed

weeks, like we do with the brunch, so we have photos and stories to go along with each theme."

"Sounds good," he said. "Let me know if you need help testing out any of the recipes. I'm a good taster."

After breakfast, Joanna and Emily set themselves up at the dining table. It was the only place big enough to spread out their cookbook-related papers and photographs, other than the floor. And Joanna wasn't keen on working on the floor.

"At my age, it's too hard to get up again," she said.

Emily opened the folder and spread everything out. Then she pulled two chairs up to the table, one for her and one for Joanna. Joanna brought them each a cup of coffee, their second for the day. Emily was trying to cut back but couldn't resist the homemade hazelnut creamer Joanna had made for them. It had just the right amount of sweetness to it but meant Emily drank far more coffee than she normally would.

"I'm going to have to buy decaf if you keep spoiling me with these creamers," Emily said. "I'm becoming an addict."

Joanna chuckled. "All part of my devious plan to keep you here, my dear."

Emily laughed at that. Joanna often made comments that indicated she thought Emily might leave. She wasn't sure why. Emily was perfectly content in her job. Perhaps it was because Joanna realised there wasn't a lot of opportunity in the role. But Emily liked being close to her sister, Wanda, who lived five minutes away. The flexibility meant she could help whenever her sister needed it. And besides, she was considering going to university. She'd never made it there, and she'd always thought about it. Now, she'd built up a little nest egg of savings and could afford to take a few classes. Maybe she would find something she was passionate about. But in the meantime, she couldn't imagine a better job than taking care of Joanna and helping her write cookbooks.

"I'm not going anywhere," she said.

"I noticed those brochures from the University of Queensland. Are you thinking of attending?" Joanna said as she moved photographs around the table with her fingertips.

Emily leaned back in her chair. "Maybe. Although I'm also looking at the University of the Sunshine Coast."

"What would you study?" Joanna asked, her head cocked to one side as she looked for something. She reached for a photograph of the Eiffel Tower and slid it down the table with a look of satisfaction on her face.

"You know how much I love taking care of people," Emily began. "I'm considering becoming a midwife. I love babies. Helping bring them into the world would be pretty amazing."

"That *would* be lovely," Joanna said. "When I had my babies, the midwives were so wonderful. They really made the experience one to cherish. I don't know what I would've done without them. And I can certainly imagine you in that role. You'd be perfect for it. Although I'd miss you here."

"It'll take me four years full-time. So, I don't know if I should do it. It's a lot to take on. I can't imagine studying full-time on top of everything else. I can't neglect you..."

"I'm sure you can manage it without neglecting me. We'll be finished with this book soon, and then you'll have a lot more time on your hands. I feel like I'm getting a little better every day, in large part because of your help. Leaving the house isn't as daunting as it was even a few months ago. As much as I hate to admit it, I won't need you so much in the future. And if you want to do something, you should at least get started. One step at a time. Don't wait, my dear. Time passes whether you follow your dreams or not. You might as well reach for those dreams while it goes by."

"That's true," Emily said. "Thanks, Joanna. I'll definitely think about it. And I'm so glad you're feeling better. That's because you're willing to take the plunge and try things."

They spent all morning working on the layout for the

cookbook and all afternoon refining recipes for the collection. By the time Joanna retreated to her room for her afternoon nap, Emily was exhausted and ready for a break herself. As soon as she'd finished cleaning up the kitchen, she carried a herbal tea out onto the back patio, with the latest thriller she was reading from the local library. She really wanted another coffee with hazelnut creamer but was doing her best to resist. So instead, she hurried back to the kitchen and grabbed a couple of freshly baked scones with whipped cream and home-made blueberry jam.

She sat with her legs tucked up beneath her, eating a scone and drinking her tea, while she read. Birds chirruped in the garden. The blue water in the pool sparkled beneath the afternoon sunlight. The sun, as it set, painted the world with a golden hue. Every now and then, Emily looked up from her book to take it all in. She should go for a walk, but she was feeling lazy. And she'd been on her feet for most of the day.

As she was reading, she heard the garage door slam shut. Aaron must be home. He kept his car in the three-car garage alongside Joanna's and Emily's. He'd bought it soon after he arrived on the island. It must be hard for him trying to establish a whole new life after years in the military. He must miss his friends. But he didn't talk about it much.

A few minutes later, he found her on the porch. He knocked on the doorframe. "Do you want some company?"

She nodded, put her book down and patted the seat beside her. "That would be nice."

He sat, leaned back and sighed.

"Long day?" she asked.

"It went quickly. I'm working on a new project for a utility. We're developing software to map water usage."

"That sounds interesting."

"I think it will be," he replied, rubbing his eyes. "But it's a big learning curve for me."

"I never thought you'd be into technology," Emily said with a smile.

"What did you think I'd do?'

"I don't know—something to do with field hockey, I guess. You were the field hockey star."

He laughed. "I don't know if 'star' is the right word. But I loved to play."

"You were definitely the star," she replied. "The whole school would go out to watch you win."

"They watched the team," he objected.

"I went to watch *you*," she said, then bit down on her tongue, her cheeks flaming. Why did she say that?

"Did you?" He faced her, eyes twinkling.

"You knew I had a gigantic crush on you back then. Don't pretend you didn't know."

He laughed. "I didn't know."

"Yes, you did. You stole my first kiss and then ghosted me. You knew."

He frowned. "What do you mean, stole your first kiss?"

"My friends and I played a game. They were pressuring me because I was turning sixteen and had never been kissed. I didn't want to do it, but they convinced me to play along. There was this kissing booth they set up at the autumn carnival down on the beach. They were charging two dollars a kiss for high schoolers. Don't you remember? It wasn't official or anything, and the adults would've freaked out if they knew. But they thought they were so smart. Of course, I wasn't going to participate. I only pretended so they'd get off my back."

"Oh, I vaguely recall that," he said.

She sighed. "I'm glad I'm so memorable for you."

"You're very memorable."

"Well, anyway, they all got kissed, and when it was my turn, I was going to pretend someone had kissed me and leave.

They weren't paying attention. They were all chattering away behind me. So, I put my lips up to the gap in the booth, where the fictional boy was supposed to be, and then you leapt out of nowhere and kissed me."

He grinned. "You puckered up. What was I supposed to do?"

"I had no idea you were there."

"I didn't know it was your first kiss. And I didn't ghost you," he said.

"You never spoke to me about it. And you left after graduation. I didn't hear from you again."

"I wasn't quite eighteen," he said with a shrug. "I didn't know how to talk to you. But I thought about you all the time."

"You did?" She found that hard to believe. He'd been the cool kid, the boy all the girls wanted to date. She was the plain girl no one ever noticed.

"I made every excuse under the sun to come over to your house, to Tristan's house, to see you."

"You were there almost every day, but you never said a word to me."

"I wanted to," he said, meeting her gaze.

The look in his eyes made her breath catch her throat. She stood to her feet. "I should start on dinner." And she hurried inside.

Chapter Eleven

When Joanna woke up from her nap, the sun was already low in the sky. She shouldn't have slept so late. Now she'd never manage to get to sleep that night. She'd be awake, staring at the ceiling, until late, and then exhausted tomorrow. When would she learn?

She heard voices on the back porch and realised Emily was out there with Aaron. They were seated close to one another, their voices low. She wasn't sure how she felt about that. They seemed to be reconnecting—they'd known each other in childhood. Was there something between them? It was definitely possible.

Aaron was twenty-five years old and starting over in life after eight years in the military; he was most likely longing to settle down and start a family, while Emily was twenty-three and had always wanted to be married with a family of her own. Her shyness meant she rarely dated. In fact, Joanna couldn't remember the last time she'd been on a date. Truth be told, they were well suited to one another. Although, what would it mean for her working relationship with Emily if she and Aaron were to get together?

As Emily's boss, she wasn't sure she liked the idea. It could mean losing her employee. As Emily's friend, she was delighted at the prospect. And after all, they were more friends than they were boss and employee. Emily had been a rock for her in recent years. Her gentle kindness was sometimes the only thing that helped Joanna through the dark times when she was having nightmares every night about the death of her husband or the fire. Emily was the soft voice of reason that brought her out of the nightmare and back into the light of the real world.

When the restaurant burned to the ground, she'd been so exhausted trying to be the head chef, to keep everything afloat without her husband to manage the place. The bank account had dwindled down to nothing; she hadn't been sure how she would manage to keep paying the staff. And then all they'd built together before his death, was destroyed. She'd lost everything. The photographs on the walls, the spacious kitchen with its temperamental stove. All of it. And in the end, it'd been the stove that was the culprit. A fitting end after the number of arguments she'd had with it over the years.

The insurance company hadn't believed her. Thought she'd burned it intentionally to get out of the financial hole she was in. It'd taken her years to recover from the trauma of it all. Her daughter, Karen, moved far away after her husband landed a job in Melbourne designing aircraft. They'd left Sunshine after their eldest, Aaron, graduated from high school. Her son, Brett, was busy with his own life. He'd had his own set of crises to manage at the time with marriage troubles and a bankruptcy for his business. So, she was left to deal with the fallout alone.

It was only Gwen and Debbie who'd carried her through it. Emily was still a teenager, living at home, at the time. Finally the insurance company had concluded it was an accident and paid her out what they owed. She'd decided not to rebuild and instead used the money as an investment for her own retirement so she could write cookbooks instead. It'd worked out well in the end, but the nightmares kept her sleep-deprived for years. And the agoraphobia increased in intensity until finally she hired Emily to help her manage.

That had been five years ago. Emily had decided not to go to university, since she wanted to stay close to her sister, and Joanna had hired her as a live-in carer. But they'd built a relationship of so much more than that. And truthfully, Joanna didn't know how she'd have managed without her.

She decided to go outside for a quick walk before dinner. She couldn't go far without her anxiety playing up, but after her discussion with Emily earlier about getting better, she was determined to work on adventuring out of her comfort zone. So, she walked around the perimeter of the yard. The sky overhead was darkening. The streetlights were coming on. Anxiety built in her gut, but she chose to ignore it and the lightheadedness that threatened. She could do this. She wouldn't let it rule her forever.

Chris was in his garden. She could see his head bobbing above the fence. He bent over, no doubt gardening. She called out to him, and he peered over the fence with a smile.

"Good evening," she said.

He raised a hand in mock salute. "What a beautiful time for a stroll."

"How's the garden?"

"It's doing okay. Although that little rain we had recently wasn't quite enough. I think another soaking would do just fine. What have you been up to today?"

"We're working on a cookbook together—me, Emily, Gwen and Debbie."

"That sounds fun," he said.

"It is. I'm really enjoying it. Even more than when I write

the books on my own. It's special to be able to share something like that with friends."

"I can certainly understand that," he replied. "I miss my workplace for that very reason."

"You miss accounting?"

He laughed. "Does that sound completely far-fetched?"

"Not at all," she replied.

"I don't miss the accounting, but I miss the office and the camaraderie. I ran a partnership with my best friend. And we had a lot of good times together."

"Where is he now?" Joanna asked.

"He passed a few years ago," Chris replied. "I sold the business soon after. My heart went out of it."

"I'm sorry to hear that," Joanna replied. "It's hard to keep going when your partner is gone. My husband was the restaurant manager, as you know. And I was the chef. And the two of us were such a good team. But without him, I floundered."

"I remember," Chris said. "You made the best barramundi around."

She smiled. "Thank you for that. I try to remember the good things. All of that loss caused me a lot of angst, and it's probably been too much of a focus for me."

"My wife used to suffer from anxiety," Chris said. "I figured out if I could distract her, she'd forget she was anxious. And then I'd take her to the beach. That always worked a treat."

"I'm sure she appreciated you for it," Joanna replied.

"I hope so. Otherwise, we walked a lot of kilometres for nothing."

She laughed. "It was good exercise."

"You're right. An accountant definitely needs that."

"It's pretty sedentary, huh?"

He shook his head. "By the end of my career, I was happy

to retire just so I could finally stretch the chair shape out of my legs." His blue eyes twinkled.

"I was a chef and mother, so I was always on my feet."

"You're probably glad to be finally getting some rest," he said.

"I most certainly am. Although sometimes... Well, never mind."

"What is it?" he asked.

"I don't want to bother you with my troubles."

"It's not a bother. I like our chats."

She sighed. "I wish I could get out more. That's all."

"I know you struggle with that. Is it still a problem?" His brow furrowed.

"It's getting a little better. The nightmares are less frequent now. I've been receiving some digital therapy, and I think it's helping."

"Digital?"

"My therapist calls me online. It's silly, I suppose. But I prefer that to going to her office, even though she's only thirty minutes away."

"Not silly at all. That seems sensible to me."

"Are you completely retired? I thought I saw you heading off to work yesterday."

He squinted into the last rays of the setting sun behind her. "Not completely. I sold my business, but the new owner gets me to come in a day or two a week. Some of my clients have been with me a long time and weren't happy about the change. So, I keep them happy, and it gives me something to do twice a week."

"That's a good arrangement," she said. "I'm still writing cookbooks, but I'm not sure how much longer I'll do it. I can't imagine retiring, personally. What would I do with my days? Besides, I love what I do. I still can't believe I'm lucky enough to write recipe books for a living."

He grinned. "You're living the dream. So, why stop?"

"That's exactly how I feel," she replied.

Chapter Twelve

"Templeton wants to see his hourly breakdown for the month," Debbie said into the intercom on her desk.

Her assistant, Evelyne, responded immediately. "I'll put the report together and send it over. Do you want me to copy you on the email?"

"Yes, please," Debbie replied.

She pressed the button to end their conversation and returned her attention to her computer screen. She'd been in court all morning and now had to catch up on emails and admin work before a client meeting. It was a busy day and didn't look like it was slowing down anytime soon. Although she'd asked Evelyne not to book further appointments after three. She had a plan for seducing her husband tonight, and she didn't want anything getting in the way.

Debbie opened the file on the Templeton case. They were suing a client for breach of contract. It was a straightforward case, but Debbie's mind kept wandering as she ran over the facts. She found it hard to focus. Normally, she had no difficulty keeping on task. She was driven—everyone she worked with said that about her. Driven, ambitious, smart, calculated, and probably a lot of other not-so-nice things.

She'd made a lot of friends over the years and more than a few enemies. It was the nature of her business. But she wondered if it was worth it now that she was coming to the tail end of her career. She'd missed out on so much, and what did she have to show for it? A company she'd have to sell at some point in the near future, and a group of colleagues who would likely call and email for a while but would move on with their lives once she wasn't part of their day-to-day.

Was she being morbid? Probably. Things weren't so bad. She had a lovely condo. A beautiful weekender in Sunshine and her childhood friends. It was more than many could say. Her thirties had been more difficult—that was when everyone around her was having babies. And it was all they could talk about. Pregnancy, labour, child rearing—every conversation revolved around the same topics. And she had nothing to add. In fact, all she wanted to do was to hide away. And most of the time she did, in her work. She didn't want to tell people about her miscarriage. Only Gwen and Joanna knew about that.

To everyone else, she was the career-driven woman who hadn't made time for a family. And now it was one of her biggest regrets. They shouldn't have waited so long to try. Or maybe they hadn't tried hard enough. She hadn't gone down the IVF path. They'd both agreed their lives would be full enough without children. But maybe they'd made the wrong choice. She couldn't help being envious of her friends' over-flowing lives, their grandchildren, the big family holiday gatherings. Especially now that Caleb barely spoke a word to her even when they did spend time together.

After her meeting, she hurried home. The condo was quiet and dark with all the draperies pulled shut. She opened them up, and the afternoon sun flooded the apartment. It covered half of the tenth floor and was far bigger than the two of them needed. But they'd bought it three decades earlier, and it had been a steal at the time. Now it was worth a small fortune, although Debbie didn't think much about money or real estate value these days. They had more than they needed, she knew that. Otherwise, she left their financial management to her husband. She had enough to deal with managing her business.

She changed into a pair of slacks and a silk blouse, then donned an apron and tied it neatly around her trim waist. With a few deft sweeps of her hairbrush, she pulled her bob back into a clip and out of her face. She selected a soft folk album by Sarah McLachlan to play over the sound system. Then she reached into the refrigerator for the roast beef she'd stashed there the previous afternoon. It was far too big for the two of them—they would eat the leftovers for days.

With the roast in the oven, she sliced up potatoes, pumpkin, sweet potato, carrots and turnips and drizzled olive oil over them before seasoning with salt and pepper. Then she placed the roasting pan on the top shelf of the oven.

While she made the peas and corn, onion gravy and bread rolls from scratch, she opened a bottle of red wine and sipped it. Slowly the kitchen filled with the delicious scents of roasted meat and vegetables. Debbie danced to the music, her wine glass raised high in the air. She felt alive for the first time in a long time, really alive. She was going to save her marriage. She'd thought about it a lot in recent years — should she leave him? Look for a man who saw her? Who appreciated her? Or should she fight to save what they had?

When they'd married thirty years earlier, they'd had hearts full of dreams. They'd loved each other so much, she almost couldn't stand it. Hated to be away from him. Couldn't stand it when he travelled for work. And when they were together,

her heart was full. But in recent years, she felt as though she was an afterthought for him. Someone he stayed with out of duty. He was polite to her, kind even. He kissed her on the cheek when he left for work. He told her his schedule, most of the time. But the passion had drifted out of their relationship like air from a balloon.

That was normal. Wasn't it? Of course it was. Passion faded for everyone. But shouldn't there still be something more than this? This shell of a relationship that they had between them didn't seem enough to stay for. And yet, she couldn't leave. She remembered how it'd been between them, and she wanted that back. There must be something she could do.

By the time the roast was cooked, the entire condo was filled with the delicious scent. She poured two glasses of red wine and set them on the table. Then she set their places with her favourite china pattern and sparkling silverware. She waited at the table for a while, but he didn't come home at his usual time.

Fingernails tapping on the glass tabletop, she glanced at the front door repeatedly until finally she decided to call him. He didn't answer the phone. She hung up and stared at the screen. Now what? Maybe he was driving. He would be home soon. He hadn't said anything about being busy tonight— she'd made certain of that. She'd asked that morning if he had anything on after work, and he'd said no, he'd be home at the usual time.

Where was he?

* * *

Two hours later, the roast looked dry. Debbie shut the oven door with a sigh, then leaned on the counter and sipped the last of her wine. She'd tried calling Caleb five times; each time, the call had gone directly to voicemail. He must have seen the missed calls. But he hadn't texted or returned her call. Something was wrong. Maybe he'd been in an accident. Panic rose up her throat. She should call the office and check when he left.

She picked up her phone just as the front door swung open. Caleb pulled his key from the lock and glanced up at her in surprise.

"Oh, I wasn't expecting to see you. I thought you'd be watching something on TV by now."

She walked over to kiss him on the cheek. There was a touch of stubble and the faint scent of his cologne. "I was waiting for you. I thought we could have dinner together."

"Oh, sorry, I already ate. I had a late meeting at the office, and we ordered some takeaway. I hope you didn't cook."

"I made a roast."

He frowned. "You did? You haven't done that in a long time."

"I know—I made an effort. I thought you were coming home."

"Again, I'm sorry," he said. "You should've called."

"Check your phone," she replied.

He pulled it out of his briefcase. "I must've had it on mute."

"Never mind. I'll eat dinner myself and put the rest away for tomorrow." She spun on her heel to walk back to the kitchen, feeling deflated.

He didn't follow her but instead retreated to the bedroom. Most likely to shower and change. It was his daily routine. She sat in the kitchen with a plate of almost-cold roast and ate by herself. Then she washed the dishes and padded to the bedroom to get into her PJs.

Her throat ached with unshed tears. Was this the end for them? He didn't seem to care that she'd put work into a meal and he'd missed it. Was she expecting too much of him?

He was in the media room. She could hear the television set. The widescreen was set into the wall with armchairs placed in rows on an incline in front of it. She peeked in through the doorway. He sat in one of the armchairs, which was big enough for two, with his feet up on the footrest. A football game played on the screen. The players were life-sized.

The sight of him tugged at her heartstrings. The grey in his hair wasn't as visible in the dim lighting, and from this angle, he looked like the young man she'd fallen in love with. He leaned forward, hunching over his knees to watch the game, then leapt to his feet with a shout, pumping a fist in the air.

She smiled to herself, then joined him. She curled up next to him in the love seat. He peered down at her in surprise and moved over. She shimmied closer again. He seemed tense. Maybe he was stressed from work. He never talked about it; she had no idea what he was up to when he was at the office. He was a barrister, like her, but he worked with bigger clients and larger dollar amounts. It must get to him sometimes, but she didn't know, since he'd never gotten into the habit of sharing.

"How was work?" she asked.

"Huh?" His eyes never strayed from the screen.

"Did you have a good day?"

"Fine."

"I left work early," she said.

"Wonders never cease."

"Maybe you could cut work tomorrow, and we could do something together. We haven't done that in a while, and I have the day off."

He frowned. "I can't just take a day off. I've got meetings. People depend on me."

"I know that..." She sighed. "It was an idea, that's all. Maybe you could plan a day off."

He didn't respond.

His shoulder was hard beneath her cheek. She raised a hand to stroke his chest. But he leapt to his feet again with another shout, then swore at the television screen. With an ache in her heart, she got to her feet and walked out of the room. He didn't say a word.

Chapter Thirteen

The grass was wet with dew as Emily tiptoed across it. The sun was low on the horizon, and birdsong rose in a chorus to welcome the new day. The cool air felt good on her bare skin. Goose pimples made bumps along her arms. She stood at the front door of her sister's small single-story, three-bedroom home and knocked quietly.

Inside the house, she heard a squeal, followed by a thump and the thunder of little footsteps as they charged at the door. She smiled to herself, imagining the bedlam inside.

The door was flung open, and two sets of little eyes peered out at her followed by wide grins and shouts of delight.

"Shhh..." she said, stepping through the doorway.

She scooped Mia into her arms as Mason jumped up and down in protest. Planting kisses on Mia's plump cheeks, she shut the door behind them, hoping the neighbours were already awake.

"Where's Mum?" she asked Mason as she bent to set Mia back on her feet and to give Mason a hug.

He shrugged.

Just then, Wanda strode into the kitchen. "Oh, Em, you're here. I didn't hear the door."

"The kids let me in."

Wanda frowned. "You're not supposed to answer the door. I've told you that."

"It's okay..." Emily began.

"No, it's not. What if there was a bad person on the other side? Mason? Do you hear me?"

Mason had already run off with a shout and disappeared into the small formal dining room that Wanda had turned into a playroom.

Wanda sighed. "You don't know how glad I am to see you. Tea?"

"I'd love one," Emily said. "But you sit and put your feet up. I'll make it."

Emily exchanged places with Wanda, who sat at the kitchen table with a groan and rubbed one foot with both hands. "My feet are killing me. Ever since I was pregnant with Mia, I've had these terrible aches in my feet."

"You should get that looked at."

"After the million other things I have to do and pay for... Sure, I will get right onto that." Wanda grimaced.

Emily filled the kettle with water and flicked on the switch. Then she began the search for two mugs.

"You said you had the morning off?" Wanda asked.

Emily nodded. "Joanna has an appointment with the physiotherapist, so she said I could take the morning. I thought it'd be nice to hang out with my favourite sister."

"Your only sister," Wanda replied.

Emily grinned. "True, but still my fave."

Wanda laughed. "I don't know what I'd do without you. Speaking of which, do you mind if I pop out in a few minutes? I've got to run some errands, and I'd really love to do it without the kids. They drive me crazy. I can hardly keep up with them these days. They both run in different directions as soon as I let them out of the car. It's like they've got a pact or something. A pact to make me lose my mind."

Emily swallowed her disappointment. She'd hoped to spend the morning catching up with Wanda. As much as she loved her niece and nephew, she missed spending time with her sister, just the two of them. It seemed every time she came over, Wanda found an excuse to leave her with the kids. And she understood—Wanda was tired, overwrought. She'd been a single mother now for twelve months, and it was hard. Her boyfriend had run off to the mines before Mia was born, leaving the three of them to cope alone.

"Have you heard from Brian?"

There was a glint in Wanda's eyes. "No. I'm not going to. He left to make more money in the mines—that was his excuse. Said he wanted to take better care of us. But we haven't heard from him since. I tried calling... His parents say he's fine, but they won't talk about him any more than that." She looked down at her hands. "I don't know what I did wrong."

"You did nothing wrong," Emily said as she dropped tea bags into the cups. "He's the one who left his family behind."

"I didn't see it coming."

"I know you didn't," Emily replied with a sigh. "But you can do this. You're strong and capable. And you've done so well this past year. The kids are happy and healthy—that's the main thing."

"I guess. Although it's lonely."

Emily knew what she meant. Sometimes she wondered if she'd ever find a person to share her life with. She hadn't been on a date in so long, it made her chest ache to think about it.

"It won't always be like this. You're in the trenches. At least your chemo is over." Emily filled the mugs with boiling hot water and carried them to the table. She set one cup in front of Wanda, then sat across from her.

"Yes, at least I'm in remission. And I'm really grateful for that. I am. I don't know what the kids would've done..." Her voice trailed off.

Emily reached out a hand to squeeze Wanda's forearm.

Mia hummed and played in the corner with a set of blocks. In the playroom, Emily could hear Mason throwing something against the wall. She hoped it was a ball.

"It feels like it'll be this way forever. And how will I find someone else when I have two...?" She dipped her head in Mia's direction. "Two angels... But it makes it hard." Her eyes filled with tears.

"There's someone out there for you. Someone who won't run off the moment things get hard." Emily hoped with all her heart that was true. For herself and for Wanda. She didn't want to go through life alone. All she'd ever wanted was a family—a husband, children to take care of. She knew her sister felt the same way. And she'd almost had the life she wanted. But Brian hadn't wanted to get married, then he hadn't wanted their second, unexpected pregnancy, and then he'd left without warning. Their simple dreams seemed impossible some days.

"Thanks, Em." Wanda reached out to squeeze her hand.

* * *

Once the sun had risen, the day grew hot quickly. Emily decided to take the kids to a nearby playground by the beach. It was the best way to tucker them out and to keep them from trouble. Being in the house with them generally meant someone was up to mischief and someone else was crying. So, she packed a small bag with waters, snacks, wipes, nappies and anything else she could think of.

The three of them headed out with both kids in an enormous, unwieldy pram. But it was better than having Mason run wild in every direction. At least with the pram, she could strap him in and be certain he wouldn't dart into traffic. He hadn't wanted to get into the pram. He said three years old was a big boy and he didn't need to be in the baby carriage. But she'd insisted, and thankfully he'd complied without too much trouble.

At eighteen months of age, Mia was easier to manage, although she would often hurt herself. She hadn't been walking long and would bump into things or fall. It was a relief to be striding down the footpath that paralleled the beach, the breeze in her hair, and both kids happily chattering away in their respective seats.

The playground was nestled in the shade of an enormous fig tree. Emily slathered the kids in sunscreen anyway and then set them down in the sand. Mason immediately ran towards the slide, while Mia trundled towards a plastic wall with moving parts. Emily followed close behind her and watched her play.

A surfer jogged down the footpath towards them. He turned to head along the walkway to the beach, then stopped and looked at Emily. She recognised him with a jolt. It was Aaron.

"Oh, hi," she said, giving him a wave.

He jogged over to her and set his surfboard down on the grass. His wetsuit was zipped up but dry. He must have only just arrived.

"I didn't realise you were down here," he said. "I thought you were at your sister's this morning."

"I thought you were at work," she replied with a laugh.

"I'm working from home today."

"That sounds nice."

"We're giving it a try. My boss is big on flexible work arrangements." He ran his fingers through his hair, making it stand on end. It was longer than it had been, and it suited him.

"Well, I'm watching Wanda's kids for her while she runs some errands." She looked at Mia, who had plopped onto her bottom and was pushing sand into a pile.

"That's good of you."

She shrugged. "I love the kids. They're a lot of fun. Although I would like to spend time with my sister too. I know she finds it difficult to get things done, since she's on her own."

Aaron climbed over the low pole fencing and joined her in the sand. He crouched down in front of Mia and helped scoop sand. She grinned at him and asked him a hundred questions, which he answered patiently. Emily watched with interest.

Soon Mason came careening over to them begging for help on the swing. Aaron immediately volunteered to push, and the two of them headed off. Emily helped Mia with her sandcastle while watching out of the corner of her eye as Aaron pushed Mason higher and higher, much to his delight.

Before long, both kids were chasing Aaron around the playground, squealing. He feigned tripping over and landed in the sand with a grunt. Both kids piled on top of him, laughing and pummelling him at the same time. He was a natural with them. And they liked him immediately. This was a side of him that Emily had never seen before. He usually seemed so serious, and in high school had been downright brooding. But this lighthearted, fun side of him was appealing. He'd be a good dad one day. A quality she found extremely attractive.

When he finally rose to his feet, his wetsuit was covered with sand. As Emily strapped the kids into their pram and handed them a drink and a snack, he brushed himself off.

"Thanks for helping with the kids. They had a ball," Emily said.

He smiled. "I love kids. They make everything fun."

She laughed. "I don't think my sister would agree with you on the word choice, but I know what you mean."

"It's difficult doing it on your own, I'm sure."

"She's struggling," Emily admitted. "But I help her out as much as I can."

"You're a good sister." He stared at her with intensity in his gaze, a slight smile on his face. She felt her heart rate accelerate.

"I try."

"Have you heard from Tristan lately?" he asked.

Aaron and her brother had been best friends in high school. "Yes, he's doing well down in Melbourne. He's married now. Did you know that?"

"I heard," he replied. "I couldn't make it to the wedding. I was overseas."

"I remember you being away," she said.

"Tristan and I had a bit of a falling out," he said. "We haven't spoken in years."

She didn't want to pry. "Oh, I thought something must've happened. You two used to be inseparable."

"Yeah, it was silly, really. But then again, I suppose most fights are."

"What was it? If you don't mind me asking... You don't have to say."

He looked down at his hands. "He was supposed to sign up with me. He backed out at the last minute and left me to join on my own. I was angry." He shrugged. "I'm over it."

"I didn't realise that," Emily replied. "He never told me he was going to join the military."

"It was our plan, both of us. We were going to do it together. I couldn't believe he backed out and didn't tell me until I'd already joined. I was angry with him for a long time."

"I can understand that, I guess." It wasn't out of character for Tristan. He was always changing his mind and flaking out on things.

"It's all in the past. I was thinking of giving him a call." He looked up at her, his eyes searching her face for answers.

"I think he'd like that," she said. "It was a long time ago, and I'm sure you've both put it behind you. You were so close —there has to be a way to reconcile."

He smiled. "You're always the optimist."

"You should give him a call."

"Thanks. I will," he said. He picked up his surfboard and settled it beneath his arm. "I'll see you later, back at the house."

She nodded and watched him jog away. Then she pushed the kids back home, unable to get the picture of him looking into her eyes with that earnest gaze out of her mind.

Chapter Fourteen

Two weeks later, Gwen was packing a picnic basket for a family trip to the beach. She made egg salad and ham and cheese sandwiches, packed dill pickles and potato salad, and also included a tossed salad, a kale salad with bacon bits, and a pasta salad. Then she added a banana cake with cream cheese frosting, an apple and rhubarb pie fresh from the oven, and a packet of ice creams, which she packed around with cold bricks to keep cool.

"Ready to go?" Duncan asked, poking his head through the doorway between the garage and kitchen.

She nodded. "The esky is packed, and this picnic basket too."

"I'll grab those." He picked up the esky and carried it to the garage. Then he returned for the basket.

Gwen quickly wiped down the bench, grabbed her purse and hurried after him.

It was a beautiful, warm day. The sun was already high in the sky, although it was only ten am. The children arrived soon after she'd covered two picnic tables with tablecloths and laid out the chips, dip, cheese, crackers and olives on platters. She also set up a bucket of ice with drinks cooling in it—iced tea, homemade lemonade using fruit from the lemon tree in her garden, and sodas.

"Can I have a Passito, Nanna?" one of the kids asked.

"Yeah, me too!"

There was a chorus of requests then, and she handed them out one at a time, giving hugs and kisses as she went. Ten grandchildren. It was a lot. She was grateful for every single one of them. She smiled as they trotted away to play on the playground. Their parents stood around the playground, chatting and drinking. Gwen would join them in a minute. She wanted to get the food organised first.

"You're sugaring them up?" Beth asked. Beth was her youngest and not married yet. "Glad I'm not taking them home."

"I'm their grandmother. I like to spoil them," Gwen said as she turned her attention back to prepping the table of food.

"This looks great, Mum." Beth reached for a piece of potato salad with her fingertips, and Gwen smacked her hand away.

"Use a fork!"

Beth grinned. "Sorry. I'm starving. I forgot to eat breakfast."

"How can you forget?"

"I was working."

"On a Saturday?"

"I work all kinds of hours, Mum. It's the modern age. We might work on Saturday and take off Monday. We're wacky like that."

"What are you working on?" Gwen asked as she poured herself a cup of sparkling water.

"I'm designing a whole new brand for a manufacturing company from New Zealand. It's pretty fun, actually. They've told us to use our imagination—they're open to anything."

"That sounds nice," Gwen said. "You're kind of amazing, kid. Has anyone ever told you that?"

"You. All the time." Beth laughed. "But thanks, Mum."

"How's everything else going in your life?"

Beth shrugged, picked up a chip and munched on it. "Fine, I guess. I was dating a guy, and he said he wanted to open our relationship up to other options. I told him the only option now available to him was to walk away. And he'd better do it fast because Tigger is trained to attack."

Gwen gasped. "Good for you. I can't believe he said that. What is this world coming to?"

"I don't know, Mum. I do not know. But whatever it is, it's spreading."

"How is Tigger? Has he recovered from the surgery?"

"It wasn't surgery, Mum. He was simply relieved of his ability to procreate. And he's a cat. He's fine."

"Good to hear." Gwen cleared her throat. She watched the children playing in the distance as she swallowed a gulp of water. "They're all growing up so fast."

"Hmmm..."

"Do you think about having kids?"

Beth laughed. "Mum, no. I'm still a kid myself."

"You're twenty-six years old, darling. You're not a kid."

"I feel like a kid." She nibbled another chip.

"Everyone feels like a kid at your age. You just dive in."

"Well, I haven't found the right person to dive in with. Did you not hear the story about the open relationship?"

Gwen shook her head. "Sometimes I wonder if anyone ever finds the right person..."

Beth frowned. "What do you mean? Are you okay? You don't seem like yourself today."

Gwen forced a smile onto her face. In the distance, Duncan pushed one of the kids on a swing and laughed out loud at something they said. She felt anger rise up in her gut. "I'm fine. Perfectly fine."

"That was creepy," Beth said with a shudder. "For a moment, you looked like one of those Stepford Wives."

"Thanks a lot."

"Just for a second. Are you sure you're okay? You can tell me anything, you know. We girls have to stick together in this family. We're completely outnumbered."

Where was Eva? She was only two years old. She'd been playing in the sand, building a moat with some mud she'd found beside the sandpit. Gwen had been considering getting some wipes for her face. But now she couldn't see her.

"Yes, we are outnumbered," she said absently.

"Is it Dad? Is he causing trouble?"

"No, he's fine." She lied because she couldn't tell her daughter the truth. Beth loved Duncan. She didn't need to know that he might be having an affair. And besides, Gwen wasn't sure that was even true. No need to start the family rumour mill going. "Where's Eva?"

"Huh?"

Her gaze roved over the grassy area, through the dunes and down towards the ocean. The beach was mostly empty. It was a windy day, and no one wanted to brave the massive waves besides the few surfers who sat on their boards out beyond the break.

"She was right there..." Gwen's heart fell into her gut. There was a little blonde head bobbing across the sand towards the surging waves. "Oh, no! Is that her?" She pointed.

Beth tented a hand over her eyes and squinted. "I think it is." She took off running in the direction of the pathway that led to the beach. Gwen was right behind her.

As she ran, Gwen kept her eyes firmly on the tiny head in the distance. The girl was so close to the waves, and she wasn't slowing down. Why hadn't anyone noticed her slip away?

They were busy talking, no doubt. It was so easy to be distracted in a large group. And there were so many little kids in their family that one could disappear without much trouble.

"Eva!" she shouted. "Eva! Stop!"

But her voice was whipped away by the wind. Behind her, she heard the commotion of her adult children and their spouses realising what had happened. Hilton, her second child and Eva's dad, thundered past her in a sprint. But she didn't stop running. She couldn't move quickly, and it frustrated her. Her feet dug into the sand with each step, slowing her pace.

There was a hole in the sand, and she didn't see it until the last moment. Then as her foot landed in the sand, she felt her ankle twist, and she fell to the ground with a thud. The pain in her ankle was intense. She lay on her side, groaning as she reached for her foot with both hands. Something wasn't right.

"Mum!" Brandon was at her side. "Are you okay?"

"Eva," she whimpered.

"Eva's okay. Hilton grabbed her. He's carrying her back up the beach now. What happened?"

"I twisted my ankle," she said with a sob. She couldn't recall the last time she'd cried. But the pain was so bad. Already she could feel the ankle swelling.

Brandon yelled for Duncan, and he called for an ambulance. Gwen spent the next four hours at the hospital getting X-rays and having her foot and ankle bound up and placed in a boot. She was told she'd have to wear it for at least six weeks. Finally, they sent her home, doped up on painkillers. Duncan met her in the waiting room. He hadn't stayed with her, since he wanted to be with the kids for their picnic.

"You understand," he'd said as he pressed a kiss to his fingertips and from there to her forehead.

She didn't understand at all. If he'd broken his ankle, she'd have stayed with him all day to make sure he had something to eat, to drink. To ensure he was well taken care of. She wouldn't have left his side. Instead, she'd spent the day alone with doctors and nurses, and hours of staring at blinking television screens with shows playing on them she couldn't quite hear.

He rolled her wheelchair out through the hospital and into the parking deck, then helped her into the car. She was quiet. She sat in the passenger seat staring out the window as he drove them home. He seemed cheerful. His face had a pinkish hue from too much sun.

"Did you have a nice day?" she asked.

He smiled. "It was lovely. The weather was perfect. The kids had a great time. We had a water fight, ate lunch, then all took a swim."

"That's nice," she replied, fuming beneath the surface. "Did you pack up all the food and bring it home?"

"Hmmm? Oh, yeah. I think someone did that. It's in the boot."

"You left it in the boot? In this heat?"

"I'm sure it's fine, Gwenny. You weren't there to take care of things, so what did you think would happen?"

When they got home, Duncan helped her inside, then carried all of the beach things from the car to the kitchen and set the bags and esky on the floor. Then he disappeared into his office. Gwen stood in her new boot, leaning against the counter, staring at the full bags. They were packed haphazardly, with everything twisted, bunched and thrown into them. The food was packed in containers, but the salads were too warm to keep. She'd have to throw them out.

Slowly, while limping about on her boot, she got to work unpacking everything and putting it away or throwing it in the bin. It took her an hour to get it all done. By then, she was starving, thirsty, had an enormous headache and couldn't wait to get off her foot.

She quickly ate a sandwich, drank a cup of water and headed to bed. Her throat ached with unshed tears as her thoughts whirled. She'd broken her ankle, and her husband and children hadn't thought to bring her things home and unpack them for her. They hadn't stayed at the hospital with her to make sure she was okay. They'd had a fun day together, as planned. And she was glad they'd had fun, but they hadn't considered her for a single moment.

Chapter Fifteen

Joanna hung up the phone, her face grim.

"What is it?" Emily asked as she wiped down the benchtop after their lunch things were cleaned up.

"It's Gwen. She had a fall yesterday and broke her ankle."

"Oh, no!" Emily's eyes widened. "That must've hurt."

"I think so. She's wearing a boot and finds it hard to get around. I agreed to go with Debbie to visit her."

"That will be nice," Emily said carefully.

Joanna could see what Emily was thinking. It was written all over her face. She was worried about how Joanna would go, leaving the house. She hadn't been out of their yard in weeks. But Joanna was ready to try. She wouldn't ever get well if she didn't step outside her comfort zone. And besides, Gwen needed her. She wasn't about to abandon her friend in a time of need.

"I'm going to make a casserole while I wait for Debbie to get here. She's going to drive," Joanna said.

"I'll help you," Emily said. "It's the least I can do. Poor Gwen. How horrible for her."

"Let's make a lamb and potato casserole. It'll be the perfect comfort food for her and Duncan."

"It would go great with cornbread," Emily said. "Don't you think?"

"Yes, it would," Joanna agreed. "Let's bake some. In fact, I'd love some cornbread. Let's make two casseroles and two loaves and keep one of each for ourselves for dinner tonight. I think Aaron would enjoy that."

"Great idea."

They sliced up lamb into thick chunks, along with onion, garlic and potatoes. Before long, the lamb was roasting, and the delicious scent had filled the house. While Emily worked on the vegetables and gravy, Joanna set about mixing up the loaves of cornbread.

She slipped the pans into the oven, then excused herself to freshen up in the bedroom. She changed out of her casual clothes into a pair of slacks with a silk blouse. Then she curled her hair and applied a little makeup. When she was done, she could hear Debbie's voice in the kitchen, so she hurried out to greet her.

Joanna kissed Debbie's cheek. "You made good time."

"The traffic wasn't so bad. Are you ready to go?"

"Let me put this casserole and cornbread into a carry bag, and we can leave."

She was in such a rush that she barely noticed the walk to the car. Debbie chattered on about her day as they walked and helped Joanna put the food into the back seat on the floor. Then Joanna climbed into the car and fastened her seat belt. Her thoughts were absorbed with what Debbie was saying as well as concern over Gwen's predicament.

"Did Gwen tell you anything other than that she fell?" Joanna asked suddenly, interrupting Debbie's train of thought about a client who was giving her trouble.

Debbie frowned. "Something about little Eva running for

the water and Gwen chasing her. I think she tripped in a hole in the sand."

"Ouch," Joanna replied. "That can happen so easily."

"She's a little down in the dumps," Debbie said. "Apparently Duncan and the others in her family didn't help her put away the leftovers or clean up after the picnic, even though she was at the hospital all alone."

Joanna's eyes widened. "They didn't stay with her?"

"Nope." Debbie shook her head. "I don't understand her kids. She's given her entire life to raise them, has sacrificed so much for them, but they don't seem to appreciate her at all."

"It happens," Joanna said. "They have their own lives, and they don't tend to think of Mum as a person. Although most grow out of it at some stage. Hers seem to have stuck with their teenaged worldview. She should snap them out of it."

Debbie laughed. "I agree. Although it's not really something Gwen is going to do. Is it?"

"No, that's true. She's the peacemaker of the group."

When they arrived at Gwen's big house, Joanna stepped out of the car with the realisation that she hadn't gotten anxious on the drive over. The anxiety hit her then as she made her way to Gwen's front door. But she couldn't help being a little proud of herself and worked hard to ignore the building dread in her gut.

When Gwen opened the door for them, Joanna hurried inside and felt the anxiety fade. "Oh, honey," she said. "Did it hurt?"

Gwen nodded, her lips pulled taut. "It was so painful. Thankfully, everyone was there to help. The ambulance didn't take long, and they had this lovely whistle they gave me that made me loopy but really helped with the pain."

They all laughed at that.

"I'm glad it helped," Debbie said. "Now, you shouldn't be

on your feet. Come on—let's go to the lounge room and get you a seat. Then Joanna and I can wait on you."

"That would be a nice change," Gwen said. "Duncan went to play golf this morning and left me to my own devices. I had to try to give myself a bath—that didn't go well. And then, to make myself breakfast. I'm still a bit hungry and thirsty, to be honest. I had to sit down for a while to recover after my bowl of cereal."

"You sit, and we'll take care of you," Joanna said as they helped Gwen into her favourite armchair. "Also, I brought you and Duncan a lamb casserole with cornbread for dinner, so you don't have to make anything."

"Oh, thank you. That is very thoughtful."

Once Joanna had put away the food in the refrigerator and Debbie had made them all a cup of tea and a slice of hummingbird cake she found on the counter, they headed back into the lounge room. They all sat in armchairs and ate the cake, sipped the tea and talked about Gwen's experiences the day before.

"I'm sorry your family didn't think to take better care of you," Joanna said. "Next time, just call us. We'll be there in a flash."

"I can't believe I skipped our monthly brunch for this." She waved a hand at her big blue boot.

"We had a nice time," Joanna said. "But it wasn't the same without you."

"We ate Bangladeshi food," Debbie said. "Not my favourite."

"Hey!" Joanna objected.

"You did a great job," Debbie said with a laugh. "But it's just not my style. Sorry."

"I guess that's okay. We all have our preferences."

Joanna looked at Gwen. She seemed so sad. She was

staring at the empty plate in her hands. Joanna reached out to take it from her and set it on the coffee table.

"You okay, hon?"

"Not really. I'm at the end of my rope with Duncan. I should've asked him about the perfume. But I'm not sure I want to hear what he has to say."

Debbie reached out to squeeze her hand. Gwen looked up at her with a grateful smile.

"What if he says he's in love with someone else? Or that it's over? I don't have anything without him. This house, our family—it's all I've got. If I leave him, what will I do?" Tears rolled down her cheeks.

"Are you thinking of leaving?" Joanna asked.

She nodded. "I have to. I can't stand him right now. Can't stand hearing his voice, looking at him. I'm so angry with him. He abandoned me at that hospital all alone for four hours when I was high on painkillers and had a broken ankle. I was scared, and they left me lying there for so long. I didn't know what was going on. I had to pee, and I was hungry and thirsty. There was no one there for me." She sniffled. "Am I being unfair?" She looked from Joanna to Debbie with the question written on her face.

Joanna shook her head. "You're not being unfair." She was angry too. Angry that Duncan would treat his wife that way after everything she'd done for him over the years.

"I'm so sorry that happened," Debbie said. "Maybe you two need a little space from one another. Don't make any rash decisions yet. But you could take a break. Come and stay with me for a night or two. Give yourself a little room to breathe."

Gwen wiped her eyes with her fingertips. "That actually sounds good."

Chapter Sixteen

Debbie tiptoed to the door of the guest room and peeped inside. The room was decorated in the modern style with a grey quilted bed, silver bedside lamps and blue curtains that matched the blue print wallpaper on the opposite wall. Gwen was already awake, sitting up in bed with a book in her hands. Her greying hair was mussed. She had dark smudges beneath her eyes. She looked tired. She smiled at Debbie, who yawned.

"Did you sleep okay?" Debbie asked.

Gwen nodded. "This bed is divine. Thanks so much for having me. This is just what I needed. To get away for a little bit, get some space, think."

"You're so welcome. I'm going to make some breakfast. Do you have any requests?"

"Anything would be amazing. But don't go to any trouble."

Debbie smiled. "I love cooking. Don't you know that?"

Gwen laughed. It was common knowledge in the group that Debbie never cooked. But maybe it was time things changed. She'd enjoyed making the roast the other night, even if it had been a waste of energy. But Gwen was here at her condo, and she wanted to do whatever she could to help her friend feel better, so she'd decided to tackle French toast. It couldn't be too hard. And besides, it would give her something to do.

It was Monday and she'd usually be at work, but she had the day off. And she was still struggling to find things to do with her time when she wasn't working. She had a lot of workaholic habits to break, and it was going to take a while to get used to this new phase of life.

She helped Gwen out of bed. Her friend assured her that she could manage on her own from there, so she went to the kitchen to get started on breakfast while Gwen washed up in the bathroom and got changed.

When Gwen joined her in the kitchen and sat down on one of the bar stools, Debbie was already frying French toast, her iPad stowed in the recipe book holder, recipe displayed on the screen.

"What are you making?" Gwen asked.

"French toast. I hope you like it."

"It smells divine. My stomach is growling." Gwen laughed. "Since when did you become Debbie Homemaker?"

Debbie rolled her eyes. "You know I'm Little Miss Domestic."

"Oh, that's right. I totally forgot all about your love of cooking."

"Fifty plus years of friendship and you don't know me at all," Debbie quipped with a wink.

Gwen giggled. Then she sighed. "I am really grateful for your friendship. I hope you know that. I don't know what I'd do without you and Jo."

"Right back at ya," Debbie said. And she meant it. Gwen and Joanna were the reason she'd managed to navigate most of the difficulties of life the way she had. Them and Caleb. And now Caleb was pulling away from her. Even thinking about that made her heart ache. She cleared her throat. "Speaking of which, I think my marriage might be over."

"Oh, no," Gwen replied. "Why do you say that? What's happened?"

"Caleb has no time for me. He's already at work this morning."

"I thought I heard him leave," Gwen said.

"Yes, he leaves early and comes home late. The other night, he said he'd be coming home, and I made a beautiful roast. He ate at work and didn't answer his phone. Then when he got home, he barely apologised and went to watch a sports game. I tried to join him, but he basically ignored me. I don't know what's wrong. He won't talk about it."

"Have you tried asking him?" Gwen's face was written with concern.

"Probably not hard enough. I keep giving him space to speak up, but maybe I need to ask him outright."

"I think you should. Men don't always know what we're thinking, if we don't say something."

Debbie scooped the golden fried toast onto plates, then carried them to the dining table. Gwen followed. She helped Gwen into a chair, then returned to the kitchen to get butter, syrup, yoghurt and some fresh tropical fruit, including mango, peaches and pawpaw she'd sliced earlier.

She sat at the table as Gwen piled her plate high with toast, yoghurt and fruit.

"Of course, I should take my own advice. I haven't spoken to Duncan yet either." Gwen's phone rang in her pocket, and she pulled it out. "Speak of the devil."

She answered. "Hello?"

Debbie returned to the kitchen to give Gwen some

privacy. She made them each a cup of tea, then carried it back to the table when she heard Gwen hang up the phone.

She set a cup in front of Gwen then returned to her own seat. "How did it go?"

Gwen's eyes were red-rimmed. "He asked where I was. I told him I was staying here for a while. He said that's fine, he's off to work, goodbye. So I stopped him and said, 'I needed some time away from you.' He asked me why, and I told him that he and the kids didn't take care of me when I needed it—that they all take me for granted."

"Good for you. Did he say anything else?"

"He said I was being emotional and he doesn't know what I'm talking about, that he always takes good care of me."

"Emotional?" Debbie shook her head in disgust.

"Then he had to go. He didn't want to be late. Said we could talk more later."

They ate their French toast and chatted about the progress they were making on the recipe book and what they'd cook at the next brunch. Debbie said she might even contribute a dish this time, one that wasn't from a bakery. And then Gwen's phone rang again.

This time when she hung up the phone, she was smiling nervously.

"Who was that?" Debbie asked as she ate the last bite of toast.

"That was the Surf Club. They run that fundraiser ball every year, and the organiser has backed out last minute. They wanted to know if I'd organise the ball. It's in less than a month."

"It's not very long to pull together an event like that."

"No, it's not. But I told them I'd do it."

"With your broken ankle?"

"What else am I going to do? It'll give me something to occupy my time. And besides, I've always wanted to be involved. That's why they called—I put my name on the list to help out. I didn't know they'd want me to be in charge and plan the whole thing. But I think I can do it."

"I know you can," Debbie replied. "You're exactly the right person for the job."

Chapter Seventeen

Everything was ready for the potluck brunch. Joanna was in her room getting dressed. The scent of freshly baked herb bread, pasta and wine drifted into her bedroom, and her stomach grumbled with hunger. She heard Debbie and Gwen arrive together and hurried out to greet them.

"There's our favourite chef," Debbie said as she kissed Joanna's cheek.

"How's the ankle?" Joanna asked, embracing Gwen.

Gwen shook her head. "It would be painful if I didn't have these lovely white pills to take."

"Hey, don't go getting addicted to those," Joanna said. "I've heard it can go badly very quickly."

"I'll keep that in mind." Gwen hobbled in her boot over to the nearest couch and sat down.

Joanna bustled about the kitchen putting the finishing touches on each item. Emily carried dishes to the dining room.

"I'm sorry I couldn't do much this time for decor," Gwen said with a sigh. "But I did bring a few Italian flags for us to hang."

"I'll do that," Debbie replied, grabbing the bag full of flags from Gwen's grasp. "You relax."

"Never mind," Emily said. "As long as you're taking care of yourself. We've got the brunch covered today."

"Emily is right," Joanna added. "Italian food needs no embellishment."

"It smells amazing, Jo. You've outdone yourself. And drumroll, please..." Debbie smiled, pulling an insulated bag out from beneath the bench. "I made tiramisu for dessert."

Joanna beamed. "From scratch? You made it yourself?"

"I did. There were a few missteps and some confusion about types of cream, but I got there in the end. I think it's going to taste pretty good."

"I can't wait to eat it," Emily said. "One of my favourite desserts."

Debbie got her camera out and took snapshots while the ladies found their way to the dining table. Joanna was proud of how it had turned out. The table looked lovely. It was decorated in red, white and green. In fact, it looked a little like Christmas, but the flags placed in small vases around the table helped focus the theme.

There were traditional margherita and marinara pizzas topped with sauce and fresh mozzarella, tomatoes and oregano and drizzled with olive oil. Bowls of pasta—carbonara, bolognese. Pork ragu nestled in a bed of creamy polenta. A large caprese salad with fresh tomatoes in a variety of sizes and colours, sliced mozzarella and dotted with basil leaves. Freshly baked herb bread lay on a wooden cutting board, with a bowl of whipped garlic butter beside it. Joanna's stomach growled again. She hadn't eaten a thing all morning—she'd been so busy getting everything ready. And she was excited to sit and enjoy this feast with her friends. But first, she would get them drinks.

"Negroni? Wine? We have white and red..." she trilled.

Debbie and Gwen asked for negroni, and Emily wanted a white wine. Joanna decided to try a negroni as well, since she hadn't drunk one in years. She added orange peel and ice cubes and took a sip before sitting down. The intense flavour was mixed with sweet, fruity notes.

Each of the ladies sipped at their drinks.

"This is lovely. Thank you," Debbie said.

"I think we should have a toast," Gwen said. "To the Sunshine Potluck Society and friendships that last a lifetime."

"Cheers!" they all chimed in as they clinked their glasses together.

* * *

"Where's Aaron today?" Gwen asked as they each ate the last bites of tiramisu.

Joanna's stomach was so full, she wondered if she'd be able to waddle away from the dining table. "He's at work."

"How's the new job?" Debbie asked.

"He seems to be doing well. I was pleased he found something so fast. But then again, there's always demand for computer science professionals. At least, that's what he tells me." Joanna reached for her espresso cup and swallowed the last small gulp.

"Whatever happened to that lovely girl he was dating a few years back?" Gwen said. "The one with the red curls."

"Oh, yes. You mean Rachel. She was lovely. But I don't think she liked the distance. He was posted in Darwin and spent some time in Afghanistan and then Canberra. He moved around a lot. She didn't want to do that, since she was studying for her PhD in Brisbane, I believe. And the separation became too much for them."

"That's a shame," Debbie added. "Although I completely

understand. It's so hard on a couple when they aren't able to connect."

Just then, Debbie's phone rang. She answered it and stepped out of the room. She'd been taking calls all morning. Something to do with an emergency at the office.

"I'd hoped you might be able to manage this without me," she said as she walked away. Joanna couldn't hear the rest of her conversation.

"Poor Debbie," Gwen said. "It seems like owning a business makes work never ending."

"I'm afraid you're right," Emily said. "She's been on her phone all morning. And this isn't the first time. She wants to slow down, but I don't see how she'll manage that."

Joanna shook her head. "Does anyone need anything else? I'm not sure I can move to get it for you, but I'll try."

Emily laughed. "Let's go to the den and relax. These chairs are getting hard."

They all wandered to the den and found comfortable chairs to relax in. Joanna pulled out a knit blanket Emily had made for her the previous Christmas and pulled it up over her legs. She admired the stitching and the colours.

"I love this blanket, Em. You really have an eye for design."

"You think?"

"Definitely. Maybe you should consider studying fashion design."

Emily laughed. "I don't know about that."

"No, really, I mean it."

"Thank you, Jo. Gwen, can I get you something to rest your foot on?"

"This cushion is just fine, Emily. Thank you, though."

Joanna used a remote control to set the stereo to play soft background music.

"I don't think I've ever eaten so much in my life," Emily said. "Your Italian cuisine is to die for, Jo."

"There's something special about Italian food, isn't there?" Joanna asked.

"Absolutely divine. Duncan would've loved it." Gwen's mood turned sombre.

"How is Duncan?" Joanna asked. "Was he worried when you didn't come home?"

Gwen shrugged. "He hardly seemed to notice. He called but wasn't upset when I told him I was staying over at Debbie's. If I moved out, I'm not sure he'd realise for weeks. The only thing that would give me away is that his laundry would stay in the hamper and not magically appear clean and hanging in his closet." She laughed, but the sound was hollow.

"What do you two do when you want to get away and have some time together?" Emily asked.

Gwen's eyes narrowed. "Hmmm... That's a good question. I can't remember the last time we did anything like that. But we used to go bushwalking. That was a long time ago. Now, we mostly live separate lives. He's at work, or golfing, or spending time with his colleagues and friends. I'm at home, or with the kids and grandkids, or here with all of you."

Debbie came to join them, her cheeks red. "I'm sorry about that. But apparently they're incapable of making it work without me, and there's a client emergency that I really need to deal with. I'm afraid I'm going to have to cut our time short."

She went to each of them to hug them goodbye. "It was delightful, as always. I can't wait to see how the Italian pages turn out in the cookbook, but the photos I took are looking pretty good so far. I think it'll be very special."

"I'm sure it will be," Joanna said. "You do such a good job on those images, Deb. You could've been a photographer. Really, you could."

"You're too kind. Now, will someone drop Gwen home? I

drove her here, but unfortunately I have to head directly to the office."

"Yes, I'll do that. No problem," Emily said. "You go and put out your fires. We'll take care of Gwen."

"Thank you, honey. You're the best," Debbie said, blowing Emily a kiss. "Ciao, all. See you next time."

After she'd left, they were quiet for a few minutes.

"I don't know how she has so much energy," Gwen said. "I can't keep up with her. I'm exhausted just thinking about it."

"She's always been like that," Joanna agreed. "I'm going to have a nap just as soon as you leave. And she's off to save the world."

"Or at least to save her business."

"Are you going back to her place or home?" Joanna asked.

Gwen's greying curls were swept up into a messy bun. Her blue eyes were rimmed with eyeliner, and she looked youthful in a pair of denim culottes and a white T-shirt. The heavy boot on her foot stood out against her tanned leg. She thought for a moment. "I suppose I should go home. I've got to face Duncan at some point. And there's nothing to be gained by running away from my life."

"It's the mature thing to do," Joanna agreed.

"And I always make the responsible choice," Gwen said miserably. "Even when it hurts."

Chapter Eighteen

The kitchen gleamed. Emily filled a mug with steaming hot water. Tea seeped from a bag into the water. Her phone buzzed. It was Wanda.

> Mia threw up all over the bed. Mason has a fever. And I feel awful. I'm not coping.

She texted her sister back.

> I'm so sorry. I can come by later if that helps.

> There's no point. Then you'd be sick too.

> Let me know if you need anything.

> I will. Thanks.

She walked out to the back deck, set down her mug of tea and pressed her hands to her hips to inhale a large breath. The afternoon sun glinted on the surface of the pool, inviting her in. She might go for a swim to clear her head. She still hadn't quite digested all the food they'd eaten but was feeling a little better.

She'd dropped Gwen home half an hour earlier. Between them, they'd cleaned up Joanna's kitchen, and now Joanna was down for a nap. Emily wanted to do something. She itched for a bit of activity. Sometimes she wished she had more friends her own age. She loved spending time with Joanna, Gwen and Debbie, but they'd been together since kindergarten. She was a blow-in. And she was less than half their age. She needed more stimulation, some excitement, an adventure. Her life was slipping by, and she hadn't done anything yet.

She sat and sipped tentatively at the boiling hot tea. It scorched her lips and tongue. She panted for a moment, regretting her haste.

Maybe she should go over to Wanda's and check on them anyway. Even if Wanda didn't want her to. She could bring them some chicken soup. That might help them feel better. But she needed to take a few minutes to herself first, finish her tea and have a swim. Then she'd get started on the soup.

The house phone rang, and she leapt to her feet and ran into the kitchen to answer it before it woke Joanna. She'd insisted on keeping a house phone even though no one else had one. Emily had explained to her that mobile was all she needed, but Joanna had asked, "What if there's an emergency? I always turn my phone to mute and forget about it."

She had a point. When Joanna left her phone on mute, it was impossible to reach her.

"Hello, this is the Gilston residence. Emily speaking."

"Oh, hi. I'm looking for Aaron Gilston," a woman's voice said.

"Who's calling?"

"I'm Amy Sykes. He has my number."

"I'll tell him you called."

"Can you please ask him to call me back? That'd be great."

"No worries," Emily replied.

As she hung up the phone, she couldn't help wondering who Amy Sykes was and why she was calling Aaron's home number. He obviously hadn't given her his mobile number. She hadn't mentioned a doctor's surgery or a dentist's office. Clearly it was a personal call. But who was she? Was he dating already? He'd only just arrived in town. It seemed a little unfair that he'd already be going out with other women, especially when she was right here in front of him and he hadn't so much as asked her out. Why would he, though? He'd never seen her that way. Why start now?

The front door opened, and she was still staring at the phone on the bench. She startled and turned to see Aaron walking in with his laptop bag in one hand.

"Oh, hi," she said, her cheeks warming. "How was work?"

"It was fine. I still can't believe they needed me to come in on a Saturday. I hope it's not going to become the norm. I need my weekends." He grinned, the dimples in his cheeks deepening. "How was brunch?"

"It was great," Emily replied. "I can make you a plate, if you like."

"That would be fantastic. I'm so hungry I can barely think straight."

"Coming right up." She'd have to share the phone message with him, but not right away. He'd only stepped through the door seconds ago and was famished. She would give him a chance to breathe first.

While Aaron changed, Emily heated up a plate of food for him. She left it covered on the kitchen bench, then headed to her room to put on a swimsuit. It was a hot day, and although the house was air-conditioned, the moment she stepped outside, she began to sweat. The sun bored down on her head as she slathered sunscreen over her exposed skin. The red bikini she wore was a little too small. She really should go shopping for another one. She kept hoping she'd be able to drop the five kilograms she'd gained and fit back into it.

When she jumped into the pool, the cold water rushed over her. She pushed to the surface and gasped for air. Within a few moments, it felt nice, although the initial cold had made her shiver. Then she remembered the phone call. She'd have to tell Aaron about it soon or she might forget completely. And that could seem intentional.

Ten minutes later, she heard a splash behind her and turned to see Aaron surfacing. He shook his head, sending water droplets flying. Then he smiled at her. "I hope you don't mind. It looked so good, and the city was so hot. By the way, that food was the bomb."

"I don't mind at all. And I'm glad you enjoyed the meal." She pushed her long, wet hair back from her face. "There was a phone call for you a few minutes before you got home. A woman called Amy."

He frowned. "Amy Sykes?"

"That's right. She asked if you'd call her back."

"Okay, thanks. I'll give her a call when I get out of the pool."

She wanted to ask. But she shouldn't. It wasn't her business. He had every right to date. He had no obligation to her.

"Do you know her from work?" she asked.

He bobbed in the water. "I met her there, yes. But she doesn't work with me."

"Oh." She pursed her lips and concentrated on picking up stray leaves from the bottom of the pool with her toes and tossing them over the edge onto the deck.

"We had coffee."

"Oh." So he was dating her, but nothing serious. At least not yet. Still, none of her business.

"I'm not sure why she's calling. I didn't give her my mobile. I guess she looked up the number."

"That makes sense," she said. There were too many leaves. She'd never be able to pick them all up one by one. Where was the pool vacuum? She spied it over by a clump of palm trees. What was it doing all the way over there?

She climbed out of the pool and padded, dripping, to pick up the vacuum. Then she carried it back to the pool and lowered it into the water. She jumped into the pool behind it. But the vacuum didn't do anything. There must be a button to switch it on. She ducked beneath the water's surface and pulled up the vacuum. Then she resurfaced and looked for the on switch. Where was it? She hadn't looked closely at it before. They had a maintenance guy who came regularly to keep the pool in working order. Surely the button wouldn't be too hard to find.

The vacuum was heavy. She readjusted her grip. Just then, two arms enveloped her and reached for the vacuum, holding it easily aloft. Aaron's arms were on either side of her, muscular and tanned. He peered over her shoulder so his chin was almost resting on top of her head.

"Here it is," he said, pressing a button on the side of the vacuum. "I took it out to fix a blockage. Should work fine now."

He let go of the vacuum and swam away.

"Uh, thanks." Emily realised she'd been holding her breath in her throat. Her entire body hummed with energy. She was aware of every single hair, every toe, every finger, every fibre of her being. And the skin he'd touched was still dimpled with goose bumps.

She lowered the vacuum into the water, then pushed off the side with her feet to swim a lap. She swam until she was tired. When she emerged from the water, Aaron was gone. And the ache in her heart had grown.

Chapter Nineteen

Gwen had gotten the hang of walking in the boot. She managed reasonably well, and the pain was gone. The break seemed to be healing, and she was grateful to be back at home. She was alone, since Duncan was most likely still at the golf club. He usually spent the entire day there, playing eighteen holes, eating, socialising. It was his happy place. And she often joined him—she liked spending time with their friends at the club. But not today. Today, she'd spent the morning at her potluck brunch as she often did on Saturdays. And this afternoon, she intended to get to work organising the Surf Club fundraiser.

There was a lot to do. The location of the event was easy—it would be held at the Surf Club. They were raising money to support the club's life-saving efforts. The annual fundraiser provided a large portion of their budget for the year and was a must-attend event for the local business community.

It was her understanding that the woman who'd agreed to organise the fundraiser had been through some kind of family drama, and as a result, they were three weeks out with nothing done. She'd communicated a theme, *Marie Antoinette*. Gwen wasn't sure it was a very applicable theme, given the event was being held at a small-town surf club on a tropical island, but the committee had assured her the theme was non-negotiable, as it was too late to change the marketing and ticketing that had already gone out.

The food should be French. She made notes on a notepad, her foot resting on an ottoman placed strategically in front of her leather armchair. What would work? She picked up the phone and dialled Joanna's number.

Joanna answered with a sleepy voice. "Hello?"

"Hey, Jo, I'm working on this Surf Club fundraiser. It's a French royalty theme. Any ideas for the menu?"

Joanna hesitated. "Oh, hi, Gwen. I was just napping."

"I'm so sorry. Did I wake you?"

"That's okay, I needed to get up." She yawned loudly. "French food? Okay, let's see. Bouillabaisse is a traditional French soup. You can serve it with seafood, to make it coastal, and crusty bread sticks."

"That sounds delicious," Gwen replied, quickly writing it down.

"Pizzas, of course, but with creme fraiche instead of tomato sauce. They're called Flammekueche, and they're delicious. They're from the province of Alsace. Oooh... Or you could do mini quiche Lorraines. That would be simple and yummy."

"I like that idea," Gwen replied. She was starting to feel hungry. "It has to be something I can serve to over two hundred people at the same time."

"Will you do a sit-down meal or finger food?"

"Finger food would be best since the entire place will be packed."

Joanna laughed. "Oh, you're going to upset some people."

"I don't want to do that. But I'd like to have a live band, dancing. And I want to fit as many people into the club as I can, without the costs getting too far out of control. We're meant to be raising money, not spending it."

"I think that's a great choice," Joanna said. "As long as you can back it up, and I think you've done that well."

In the end, they decided on the following menu.

Cheese, crackers, bread, olives, dips and deli meats placed on grazing platters around the room.

Mini Quiche Lorraine

Mini Bacon, Cheddar and Onion Quiche

Dijon Chicken Wings

Short Rib Bourguignon

King Prawns in a Garlic Rouille

Braised Artichokes

Mini Butterscotch Soufflés

Chocolate Eclairs and other assorted pastries

It was an ambitious menu. Gwen wasn't sure they could pull it off, but she would talk to the catering staff and see what they thought of it. Of course, they'd pair it all with local wines to keep the costs down and to support local industry.

She was putting the finishing touches on an email to her contact at the Surf Club when she heard the garage door whirring open. Duncan was home. Nerves fluttered in her stomach. She'd barely spoken to him for days. She hadn't seen him since she left to go to Debbie's. Had he noticed her absence? Would he care? She'd decided to talk to him about the issues between them but wasn't sure where to begin. They needed to have a discussion, but was this the right time? She'd never been one to choose conflict. She generally avoided it as long as possible. But perhaps that approach was what had landed her here, in a marriage she barely recognised to a man who seemed not to care about her the way she did for him.

He marched into the kitchen and flung his things down on the bench as he always did. Usually she put everything away for him, but with her broken ankle, she'd hoped he might think to do a few things for himself.

When he stepped into the living room, scotch on ice in hand, he paused at the sight of her.

"Oh, there you are," he said. "I didn't see you this morning."

"I stayed at Debbie's. Remember? We spoke about it?"

His brow furrowed. "Oh, that's right. Did you have a nice time?"

She'd called it. He hadn't even realised she was gone, let alone that she was upset with him. He walked around in his own little world. Did he think about her at all?

"It was good to spend some time with her. We had the Sunshine Potluck Society brunch today as well. I thought you might come."

He sat in his favourite armchair with a chuckle. "You ladies don't want me there. I'd spoil all the fun."

"I invited you."

"Thanks, hon. But I don't see myself attending anytime soon. Who was there?"

"Debbie, Joanna and Emily. Aaron was working."

"Oh? How's he going?"

"Settling in, I think."

"Glad to hear it. He's a good man. You should tell him to come down to the club and hit a few balls. It'd be good to see him."

"Okay." She wasn't sure what to say. Where do you begin on a lifetime of grievances? She shouldn't have let it get this far. Should've addressed things as they arose. But she'd been busy raising children, and complaining seemed out of place. What did she have to complain about, really? And so they'd drifted apart, stopped communicating, and now they lived very separate lives.

Was it her fault, or his?

She didn't want to cast blame. But it took two to ignore the cracks in a relationship. And she'd played her part, even if she'd spent most of her life doing everything she could to make him happy. By burying her own happiness and letting him trample over her needs and wants, she'd helped to build the wall between them.

He picked up a book and began to read. With one leg crossed over the other, a glass of scotch on the table beside him and a pair of reading glasses perched on the tip of his nose, he looked older than his sixty-five years. They'd spent a lifetime together, yet looking at him like this, she felt she hardly knew him. But she did. She knew him well. Knew every part of him. What he liked to eat or drink. How he slept. Where he went when he was feeling stressed. The clothes that made his skin itch or the food that gave him a stomachache. She knew him better than anyone else in the entire world. But right now, he was a stranger to her. What was going on in that head of his?

"Did you miss me?" she asked.

He glanced up at her. "Huh?"

"When I was staying at Debbie's. Did you miss me?"

He smiled. "Sure, yes, of course I did."

"Would you mind if I moved in with her for a while?"

He frowned. "What? Why would you do that?"

"I'm feeling a little unappreciated."

He sat up. "Unappreciated? Why? What happened?"

She swallowed as anxiety made a ball in her gut. She hated tension, arguing. Better to leave it all beneath the surface. But the tension would merely fester. She had to get it out into the open, no matter how hard it was. "Well, you and the kids expect things of me. And you don't seem to appreciate all I do for you. When I'm gone, you barely notice. None of the kids called to check on me. You didn't realise I was upset. I don't know how to get through to you all."

He closed his book and set it on the table. "You were upset? What about?"

"When I broke my ankle, you took me to the hospital and left me there. You didn't stay to help me or make sure I was okay. You all went back to the beach and finished the nice picnic that I had set up for you. Then you didn't unpack any of the picnic when you got home. You left a huge mess in the kitchen for me to clean up, even though you knew I was in pain and on medication."

He sighed and ran his fingers through his grey hair. "Here we go. Back to this same old argument. I don't do enough around the house. Well, I work for a living, Gwen! You know that. You chose to stay home with the kids. And I've provided a very nice life for us. Don't you think?"

Her breath caught in her throat. He'd raised his voice to yell at her. She wanted to leave and hide in her room. "Yes, you've done very well. You're a good provider and a good father. I don't think that means I should never speak up about anything that bothers me, though."

"So, now you're accusing me of silencing you? Not letting you speak?" He stood to his feet. "I don't know what to say, Gwen. This is coming out of nowhere. All these accusations."

"I didn't accuse you, Duncan," she said, wringing her hands together. "Just that you don't show me a lot of appreciation for all I do around here. The kids don't either. They assume I'll watch the grandchildren for them—they don't ask. And they never say thank you. I'm tired. I raised four kids. And now I would like to have some fun. I love my grandkids, but I don't want to be their primary carer. I want to enjoy time with them, spoil them, feed them lollies and then go home. I want to travel and see the world. We always said we'd do that and we never have. You've travelled for business, but not with me. You're always gone playing golf, working, spending time at the gym or with friends. It feels as though I'm an afterthought."

He shook his head. "Where is all of this coming from? No one is stopping you from doing anything, Gwen. If you want to travel, then do it."

"On my own?" she asked.

He laughed. "I'm busy. I have work to do. I can't go flitting off around the world at the drop of a hat. But you can. So go on. Do it."

He stomped out of the room. She watched him go, a lump growing in her throat. That hadn't gone the way she thought it would. He completely misunderstood what she was saying. His defensiveness was the reason she struggled to share things with him. It always went like that—she'd share a concern, and he'd get angry and upset, assuming she was criticising him. Then the conversation would end with him storming out and nothing resolved. It was why she generally preferred to bury her feelings and wear a smile on her face instead. Conflict never got her anywhere. And now she felt even worse than she had before.

Chapter Twenty

The church bells rang out loud and clear, a happy melody under the glare of the midday sun. Debbie cupped a hand over her eyes to cut the glare and stared out at the sparkling water over the bay.

"It's a beautiful day," she said.

"Church was lovely," Gwen agreed. "I'm glad we made the effort, even though my ankle is aching a little bit from all the standing."

"I told you to sit," Debbie admonished her with a gentle pat on the shoulder.

"I know, but I wanted to stand with everyone else. The music was so uplifting."

Church in Sunshine each Sunday was one of Debbie's favourite places in the world. She left the service feeling refreshed and fulfilled, ready to tackle another week. Her husband, Caleb, stood by the church doors in a huddle with a group of his friends. All of them wore button-down shirts and slacks, their hair neatly combed. She'd always liked the way Caleb looked when he wore his Sunday best. So handsome and well groomed, without the stuffiness of the suits he donned on weekdays.

Joanna made her way carefully and slowly down the steps to join them.

"I'm so proud of you for coming today," Gwen said. "How did you go?"

"I feel good, actually," Joanna replied. "I've been getting out of the house more and more lately. And the anxiety isn't as bad as it was. I feel like I'm finally getting somewhere. My therapist has been helping me find techniques to manage my stress levels."

"Well, it's working. You're doing great," Debbie replied. She was so impressed with how much Joanna had changed in recent weeks. She'd known her a long time, and this was the most comfortable she'd seen her friend outdoors in years. The fire at the restaurant had been a turning point in her life, one she'd never fully recovered from. Until now. It seemed she was making progress towards healing.

"Let's find a seat. I don't know how long the men will be." Debbie led Gwen and Joanna over to a park bench, and the three of them sat side by side.

Gwen sighed. "That's better. Is this okay for you, Jo?"

"You should probably be at home resting," Joanna said. "And yes, it's challenging for me to sit out here in the open like this. I'm feeling a little dizzy. But it's good for me to push myself. That's how I improve."

"You're amazing, honey. I'm so happy for you. And I don't want to be at home. It's boring at home. Besides, Duncan and I had a big fight."

"What about?" Joanna asked.

"I mentioned that I felt like I wasn't appreciated. He didn't much like it. Same thing that always happens—he got defensive and yelled at me then left. He didn't come home until late. We didn't really say much to each other this morning. He's pretending it didn't happen, but he's also not speaking to me."

"I'm so sorry, honey," Debbie said. "That sounds awful."

"It was awful. But it's also long overdue. I should've spoken up years ago. And now I may have left it too late. He can't hear me, and there's such a big divide between the two of us. I don't think I even realised it was there until now."

"Do you think you can come back from this?" Debbie asked.

Gwen shook her head. "I don't know. I hope so. But I know I need time. And there's so much more we have to say to one another. I don't know how we do that when he reacts the way he does."

"Have you considered counselling?" Joanna asked.

"I've honestly never thought about it. I didn't think we needed it. I believed we had a good marriage. But now I know that I was simply ignoring the issues. We haven't had a real conversation in so long, I can barely remember it. We don't connect with one another—we simply co-exist. It didn't used to be like this. I don't know if it's normal or if there's something very wrong."

Joanna patted her hand in silence.

Debbie's throat tightened. She knew exactly what Gwen was talking about. She was in a similar place. Maybe it was the natural progression for a relationship. "I don't think it's how things should be, but I do think it happens so easily. Caleb and I haven't had a real connection in a long time either. I don't really know what to do. But perhaps Joanna is right. Maybe we all need couples therapy."

"Have you ever looked at his phone or computer? Checked his emails or phone log?" Joanna asked. "I never did that myself, but I've heard of women doing this. It might answer some questions for you without having to confront him."

Gwen grunted. "Are you joking?"

"A little...but it's still not a terrible idea. Is it?"

"It's a terrible idea," Gwen countered with a laugh. "Spying on your husband is the last resort."

"I'm probably in last-resort territory," Debbie admitted.

"You're right. I suppose I *could* take a look at his phone or emails. Maybe there's something there from the mystery perfume lady." Gwen chewed on her lower lip.

"If she even exists," Debbie said.

"Right. If she's real."

"You should do it," Joanna said. "You need to know. You're sabotaging your relationship because you think he's been unfaithful. Maybe he hasn't been. If you looked at his devices, you might be able to figure it out and have some certainty there before you confront him over it."

"I don't know," Gwen said. "What do you think, Debbie? Would you do it?"

Debbie inhaled a slow breath. "Maybe. Who am I to say? I can't even get my husband to speak to me about anything real. In fact, I could check right now. I have both our phone logs, and I also have the login to Caleb's email. He gave it to me years ago. I've never checked it because I didn't have a reason to."

"Take a look now, then," Gwen said, sitting up straight. "If you can do it, then I might work up the courage."

"I don't know about this," Joanna said. "I was partially joking. But now that you're talking about doing it, I have a bad feeling."

Debbie laughed. "This was your idea. You can't back out now."

Joanna bit down on her lip.

Debbie pulled her phone out of her purse and logged onto Caleb's email. She checked the inbox, the archive and deleted files. There was nothing there. Nothing that stood out. Everything was either junk mail or work related, plus a few family emails from his brothers and cousins.

"There's nothing in his email. Nothing I can see immediately, anyway."

Joanna and Gwen watched over her shoulders.

"If he's cheating on you, he's very good at hiding his tracks. His email inbox is even more boring than mine," Joanna said.

"All right, let's take a look at the phone log. I can't see his messages, but I can tell what numbers he's interacting with." Debbie pulled up the log and scrolled through the list. "That's his office number, those are his colleagues, that's his brother, another brother, my number, the mechanic's..." She recognised the numbers since they hadn't changed for years, and her husband always interacted with the same people. His call log confirmed what she'd believed about him forever—he was a creature of habit and loyal relationships. He had no one new in his life. She'd been worried for no reason.

She leaned back on the bench. "He's not cheating." She exhaled a long, slow breath. "What a relief."

"He's a good man," Gwen said. "I've always thought so."

"What's going on with him, then?" Joanna asked. "Why is he so withdrawn?"

"I don't know. But it's been years. I thought it would pass, but it hasn't. It's only gotten worse."

"You've got to talk to him," Gwen said.

"I feel terrible now," Debbie replied with a frown. "I invaded his privacy. I snooped. I'm not that kind of wife. I never do things like that."

"You were worried about him," Gwen said. "And it helped relieve your concerns. Now you can speak to him without being fearful that something terrible is going on."

"Don't feel bad about it," Joanna said. "It was my idea. I pushed you to do it."

"I shouldn't have..." Debbie rubbed her hands over her face. "Ugh. I've got to tell him."

"Well, I'm glad you did it," Gwen said. "You've given me the courage to do the same. Although I don't have access to his accounts, so I'll have to find another way."

"Just talk to him," Debbie replied. "I'm sure you'll find that you have nothing to be worried about as well. Duncan loves you."

"I know he does," Gwen said. "But he's so difficult to talk to. I'm not sure how to get through to him or how to get the truth out of him."

"Here they come," Joanna said in a whisper.

The men were all headed their way. Duncan, Caleb and Chris, Joanna's neighbour, all walked side by side with Aaron, who was telling them something in a very animated voice.

"We should all go out to lunch," Joanna said.

Debbie yawned. "I can't. Sorry, hon. I've got to get back to the apartment. Work tomorrow is going to be hectic, and there are some things I have to take care of before then."

"I'm feeling worn out," Gwen replied. "Next time?"

"Okay, next time," Joanna said.

Debbie stood and smiled at Caleb, who reached out his hand to squeeze her arm.

"Ready to go home?" he asked.

She felt instant relief at his touch. "Yes, I'm ready. Bye, ladies."

As they walked away, she slipped her hand into Caleb's, and he closed his grip around it. Her throat ached with unshed tears. The memory of his emails and phone log flitted through her thoughts. She felt immediate guilt but at the same time, relief that he was the man she thought he was and had nothing to hide.

Maybe counselling was all they needed. A better way to communicate with one another. Whatever it was, she should move quickly. She didn't want this barrier between them anymore; it had become a constant source of anxiety. She wanted their relationship to go back to being how it had been when they were first married—open, loving and passionate. But how would they get back to that place?

Chapter Twenty-One

With a slotted spoon, Joanna raised the golden samosa out of the hot oil and set them on paper towels to drain. They looked perfect. These were keema samosa, filled with minced mutton, yoghurt and spices. She'd also made several batches of vegetarian samosa. There were plates of samosa all over the kitchen bench. Perhaps she'd gone a bit overboard. But she wanted to get the recipe just right for inclusion in their book. And she wasn't sure yet which version to use.

Should she go with the meat-based delicacy? Or the vegetarian one? Peas or no peas?

With a frown, she reached for one of the golden-brown pastries and plucked it open with her fingertips.

"Ouch!"

"You okay?" Emily asked as she walked into the kitchen. "Wow, it smells amazing in here."

"I burned my fingers, but I'm fine. I need to know which of these to include in the book. Can you do some taste testing and tell me what you think?"

Emily's long brown hair swung from a high ponytail down her bare back. She wore a strapless summer dress with a

133

strapless bikini underneath. The two of them had gone swimming together earlier as part of Joanna's physical therapy. Now they were working on the recipe book.

Emily reached for a plate and filled it with a variety of pastries. Then she took bites out of each.

"I like the vegetarian one with peas."

"Me too, I think. I should get one more opinion, though, before I decide."

Her phone buzzed in her pocket, and she pulled it out and held it to her ear. "Yes, this is Joanna."

"Good afternoon, Joanna. It's Bobbie."

"Oh, hi, Bobbie. How are you?" Bobbie was her editor. They'd worked together for over ten years now. Joanna had a soft spot for the woman who helped her meet her deadlines and gave feedback on her recipes. She always did it with so much grace and flair. She was good at her job and kind as well, which was a rare combination.

"I'm fine, thanks. I hope you're working hard on the Sunshine Potluck Society recipes."

Joanna grinned. "Of course. I'm finalising the samosa right now as we speak."

"Glad to hear it because I need the final draft from you by Friday. Do you think you can manage it?"

"Friday?" Joanna's heart skipped a beat. That was too soon. They weren't close to being finished. She hadn't even run the final content by the other ladies yet. Debbie hadn't sent through the layout for the photographs. Gwen was so busy with the Surf Club fundraiser and everything else going on in her life, she hadn't responded to Joanna's repeated requests for approval of the decor. And Joanna and Emily still had about twenty pages' worth of recipes and anecdotes to finalise. "Sure, Friday is good. We can manage." She always said yes to her editor, even when she wasn't feeling confident at all.

When she hung up the phone, Emily stared at her wide-eyed. "What about Friday?"

"She needs the final draft by then."

Emily gaped. "What? We can't do that. We're not even close."

"We have to," Joanna said. "That's the deadline they're giving us, and they have good reason. There's an entire team of people who need to do their part after us, and they need time to do that."

"I'll call Debbie and Gwen to make sure they're ready to send through their content."

"You do that. I'm going to see if Chris can help me decide which samosa recipe we should include."

Joanna carried a plate piled high with pastries out the front door and headed across the yard and around the fence into Chris's yard. As she did so, she noticed that the panic that rose up her spine was muted. It wasn't nearly as bad as it had been in the past. All of her hard work was paying off. She could cry, but then she'd have to explain her tears to Chris. So instead, she smiled to herself and blinked her eyes a few times, then knocked on his door.

He answered with a confused look on his face. "Well, hello. I'm not used to seeing you at my front door." He opened it and ushered her inside. "What a pleasant surprise."

"I brought samosa," she said.

"Okay. That sounds interesting."

"It's an Indian food, quite delicious. I think you'll like it."

"Not spicy, is it?" He led her to the kitchen, and she put the plate down on the bench. It was a small but tidy kitchen with a grey marble benchtop. The appliances were white, and there was a round white kitchen table by a set of bay windows that looked out over his back garden.

"No, it's not spicy. Maybe a little bit of a kick. But nothing to worry about. You have a lovely house," Joanna said.

"You haven't been inside before?" Chris asked.

"It was a long time ago. I think you've renovated since then."

"Oh, yes, that's right," he replied. "I redid the entire kitchen, both bathrooms and painted. It's made a big difference to have so much white. Really opens the place up."

"I agree. It looks lovely."

"Would you like a cup of tea?"

She nodded. "Thank you. That would be wonderful."

"I'm so glad you came to visit me. I was just about to have some tea myself, and now I have company."

He boiled the kettle and got out a china teapot with little flowers on it along with two matching cups and saucers. He spooned tea leaves into the pot. Then he filled it with boiling water. He carried the pot to the kitchen table. Joanna carried the empty cups.

They sat across from one another. Joanna realised it was the first time she'd sat down all afternoon, and the relief of it showed up in a sigh.

"Oh, it feels good to get off my feet."

"I'm going to eat one of these delicious-looking parcels," Chris said, reaching for a samosa. "And if I need a drink to cut the spice, I've got one now." His eyes twinkled.

"Let me know what you think. Don't be shy. I need the truth—it's for the book."

He took a bite. She watched his expression as he ate. Finally, he spoke. "Well, that was delicious. I'll try this other one now."

In the end, he tried all three of the flavours she'd brought with her and chose the same one she and Emily had picked, vegetarian with peas. She had her answer.

As he cleaned up after their tea, she wandered through the living area looking at the photographs on the wall. There were so many images—family, friends, travel. He'd lived a full life.

He soon joined her.

"Who is this?" She pointed to a photograph of him with a woman, her back turned to the camera. He was smiling down at her, his dark hair blown in the wind.

"That's my wife, Katie."

"Oh, is it? I didn't recognise her." The woman was young, her hair pulled into a high bun with tendrils of curls loose around her neck.

"She was very young then. Me too. That was when we moved away and lived in Ballina for a while. I don't know if you recall that. You were probably busy with babies. I know we were."

"I was very busy. And I remember you being gone, but I couldn't tell you the dates. Those were full days."

"They were," he agreed. "Our thirties blew by in a whirl, and the twenties weren't much clearer."

"How are the kids?" she asked.

He shrugged. "I see them every now and then. Not as much as I'd like. But they're in the thick of the busy times, and they don't live close by, so I get it. I've thought about moving down to Melbourne to be close to one of my boys. But I never quite get around to making a decision. I love it here. Sunshine is my home and has been for most of my life. My friends are here. It's hard to choose to move away from that to a big city where no one will know who I am or care."

"I know what you mean," Joanna said. "I've thought about Melbourne myself. My daughter lives there. Her children are almost all grown now. Actually, one of them is currently living with me, as you know. Aaron is her eldest. But she moved away after he finished high school and has been down in Melbourne for several years now. It's hard to keep track."

"I want to be close to them, but at the same time, I'm not sure they'll have the room to give me much attention anyway.

And I'd have to forge a new life for myself in a strange city. I'm not sure I'm up for that." He set his hands on his hips. "Besides, I have lovely neighbours," he dipped his head in her direction, "who keep an eye on me, and friends I've known for decades. I can go to the shops for my newspaper, and the people there know me by name. I always run into someone down at the beach, or at the bowls club, and have a good old natter together. I'd miss that. Can you imagine trying to make your way around in Melbourne all alone? I know my son would be happy to have me there, but he's got work, and kids, and a social life of his own."

"That's exactly how I feel," Joanna agreed. "I couldn't expect my daughter to spend every day with me. But here, I have Gwen and Debbie, Emily and Aaron. As well as you and a whole host of other people who have made sure I've been taken care of even when my issues have forced me to be cloistered in my house for much of the past decade."

"I see you're doing better there," he said, beaming.

"Much better lately, thanks. I don't know what's done it, whether it's the therapy or supportive friends, or maybe it's that I've decided to push myself to do things I'm uncomfortable with. But whatever it is, it's working."

"Good on you," he said. "You're a wonderful woman, and more people need to have the opportunity to spend time with you. So if you can get out and bring happiness to others, then I'm all for it."

Chapter Twenty-Two

On Tuesday, Debbie spent the morning at home. She'd had a busy time at work the previous day. Most of it involved putting out fires that were lit when she was gone the previous week. She wasn't sure this part-time thing was going to work out as well as she'd hoped it would.

She sat on the couch with her reading glasses on, working her way through a spreadsheet of expenses for the month. Then, with a tick of approval, she sent it to her assistant and slouched back on the couch with a sigh. So much for a day off. But at least she'd had a chance to put together some dinner. She'd made a soup in the crockpot that morning and was hoping this time she and Caleb would have a chance to eat together.

She'd texted him; he'd confirmed he would be home. Tonight was the night. Nerves fluttered in the pit of her stomach. They'd had a nice time at church together on Sunday. They'd even shared a coffee that afternoon. She wanted to keep the momentum going. On the days she worked, she often got home so late that he'd already eaten and was downstairs working out in the gym. But now that she had a few days off per week, it was their chance to finally connect.

Once she'd finished with her admin work, she finalised the layout for the photographs to be included in *The Sunshine Potluck Society Cookbook*. She especially loved the photographs from their India-themed segment and had included a personal anecdote. The story was from the time she'd visited Chennai with a friend years earlier and had eaten at a restaurant on the coast where she'd discovered fish curry for the very first time. It'd fast become a favourite of hers. She'd also added several photos she'd taken while touring southern India. The colours and fabrics depicted in the photographs were truly breath-taking and complemented the vibrant colours of the spices and curries.

She reviewed the content in their shared account and then sent Joanna an email with her final contributions and blessings for what they'd already done. She was excited about how the book was coming together. It looked fantastic and truly inspired her to do more cooking. The beautiful recipes crafted and tweaked to perfection by her friends made her want to try.

The phone rang, and she answered it without looking at the screen.

"Hi, Debbie, it's Phil. I hope I'm not calling at a bad time."

"Hi, Phil. It's perfectly fine. How can I help you?"

He cleared his throat. "The Blue Rock account is in trouble. They're talking about cancelling our contract."

She straightened. "What? Why? What happened?"

"Sally was taking care of their latest case, a mediation due to a sexual harassment claim in the workplace. And apparently she's been late to several meetings, she gave some bad advice that cost them a lot of money, and now she's telling them to accept a deal that they're not happy with. They want you to take the lead, or they're walking."

"Why didn't I know about any of this?" Debbie asked, rubbing a hand over her face.

"We talked about it in the meeting last week, but you weren't there."

She grimaced. He liked to make little passive-aggressive digs at her over the new schedule, but she was committed to making it work. "Okay, fine. I'll talk to Sally, and I'm happy to take lead on the case. I'll set up a meeting with the client for later in the week."

"Thanks, Deb. I could've taken care of it myself, but they asked for you specifically. So I thought..."

"You did the right thing. You can call me anytime. I'm always available."

When she hung up the phone, she heard the front door slam shut. She finished touching up her makeup and hurried out to greet Caleb. He stood by the front door, briefcase slung onto the hall table as he looked over a pile of mail.

"You're a sight for sore eyes," she said, going to him and wrapping her arms around his torso.

He kissed the top of her head. "I'm still not used to you being here when I get home. It's nice."

"I made dinner," she said. "Soup and fresh-baked bread rolls."

"That sounds perfect. I'll just wash up and join you."

Debbie set up their meal on the small verandah at the back of their condo that looked out over a park. The sun hovered behind a copse of trees so that the light was dim. The air was cool. Birds chorused throughout the park. Children played and rode their bikes down the street below.

By the time she'd set the table and spooned soup into bowls to take outside, Caleb had changed. He wore a pair of jeans and a black T-shirt. Even after all these years, he'd stayed in good shape. His hair was a steel grey now, rather than the dark brown it used to be. But his green eyes were just as piercing as they'd always been. He sat across from her as she poured him a glass of red wine.

"Thank you," he said. "This is a treat."

"I wanted us to spend some time together. We've both been busy for such a long time, we don't often get a chance to reconnect." There was so much more she wanted to say, but she was doing her best to avoid blame. She didn't want him to think she blamed him for their situation. She carried the burden of their disconnect around with her daily. It was her fault as much as his. But she wanted to fix what was wrong between them. She wasn't sure yet if he was on the same page.

He didn't respond to her words. Instead, he took a bite of the soup. Then he buttered his bread roll. "It's delicious. I was hoping for something light for dinner, since we had a business lunch at that restaurant downtown with the yum cha. I ate too much." He laughed. "I've had a stomachache all afternoon."

"I'm sorry to hear that. I can get you something for it, if you like."

He shook his head. "No, stay here. I'm sure I'll be fine after eating your soup. How was your day?"

"Busier than I thought it would be. There's a lot going on at the office, so even though I was at home, I was still dealing with issues. I've got to take over a case that Sally was working on because the client isn't happy with how she's done. I'd hoped she would step up and take on more responsibility with me pulling back, but it doesn't seem as though she will."

"Maybe you should talk to her."

"I will tomorrow. Oh, and I finalised my portion of the recipe book. We've got until Friday to get the draft to our editor."

"That's great," he said with a smile. "I never would've thought the words 'I wrote a cookbook' would come out of your mouth. But here we are."

They laughed together.

"Wonders never cease," she agreed. "Although in fairness, I didn't write it. Most of it is Joanna's work. But my photos look good, I think. And I contributed a couple of stories to go alongside the recipes."

"I'm sure you've added a lot of value. I'm looking forward to reading it."

They chatted about his day and what was going on with his work. Then about his family. One of his cousins had been diagnosed with throat cancer. Finally, there was a lull in the conversation, and she felt the thump of her heart as she opened her mouth to speak.

"I thought we might talk about our relationship."

Chapter Twenty-Three

Caleb's spoon paused halfway to his mouth. "Okay."

"I'm not placing blame on anyone, but I feel as though we've had a big distance between us for a long time, and I don't know what to do about it. So, I thought it might be a good opportunity for us to hash it out. Get things out on the table." She was nervous to hear what he had to say. Did he care about saving their marriage? Was it already over?

He set down his spoon and patted his mouth with the napkin in his lap. "I've been a bit absent. I'll admit."

"I have too," she said. "We used to be close..."

"I know." He looked away, then met her gaze. "I don't know what to say."

"How do you feel? About our marriage? About us?"

"I suppose I feel empty...sad."

Her breath hitched in her throat. She hadn't expected that. "Why? Can you tell me?"

His jaw clenched. "I think it all goes back to the...baby we lost."

Her heart lurched. The miscarriage was something she tried not to think about often. It'd happened years ago. It was a part of their shared history, but not something she liked to dwell on. There was nothing that could be done about it. But even hearing the words come from his mouth made tears spring to her eyes. He'd never spoken about their loss before. He'd moved on as though nothing had happened. It'd hurt at the time, but she'd put it behind her.

"My miscarriage?"

"Yes," he said. "I was devastated." His eyes glistened with tears.

"I didn't know that," she said, holding back a sob. "You didn't say..."

"I thought if I spoke about it, you'd feel even worse. So I tried to be strong for you."

"You don't have to do that. We should talk about these things."

"And the more time passed, the sadder I felt. We didn't get pregnant again. And then you said that it was probably for the best, that we weren't meant to be parents. You laughed about it." He blinked, and a tear ran down his cheek.

Debbie couldn't bear to see him cry. She couldn't recall him ever crying before in thirty years of marriage. Her throat constricted painfully. "I'm sorry. I was trying to be strong for you as well. I didn't mean it to sound that way — I wanted a baby."

"You did? Because I thought you were happy we didn't have one. And I guess I've resented you ever since. I didn't mean to. I didn't set out to feel that way. It just happened. I tried to forgive you and move on. I worked hard at our relationship, at least for a while. But in recent years, I haven't had it in me."

Tears fell down her cheeks. She never imagined that there was so much pain beneath the surface of his indifference. It all made sense now.

She reached for his hand. He squeezed hers. "I'm sorry,"

she said. "I wanted that baby more than anything else in the world. I was sad too."

"I'm glad to hear that."

"I wish you'd said something."

"I didn't want to hurt you," he replied. "And then I got to the point where I thought it wouldn't make any difference and there was no reason to bring it up."

She moved to kneel in front of him. He wrapped his arms around her shoulders and pulled her to his chest. She sobbed against his T-shirt.

"Do you think we can get past this?" she asked, looking up at him with tears blurring her vision.

He smiled. "Do you want to? I know I've been difficult..."

"I don't want to lose you," she said. "I love you more than anything."

"I love you too, honey. I want to make it work."

Debbie's heart swelled. It was everything she'd wanted to hear from him for so long. They shared a pain that'd been so hard to bare neither one of them had faced or processed it the way they should've. Instead of turning against one another, they should've leaned on each other. But they couldn't change the past. All they could do was try again. And she was grateful now they'd have that chance.

Chapter Twenty-Four

Gwen sat with her foot propped up on the ottoman in front of her favourite leather armchair. She had a cup of cappuccino perched next to her. She tapped on the keyboard of her laptop as she wrote up the VIP guest list for the Surf Club fundraiser. Then she took a sip of coffee.

Duncan had stayed home from work for the first time in as long as she could remember to help out around the house. It was a miracle. He'd actually heard what she said, even though he'd argued against her. At that moment, he was in the kitchen washing the dishes. She could hear the clink and clank of pans as he set them in the dishwasher. She resisted the urge to check that he was doing it right. That would only infuriate him. And it didn't matter. He'd have to figure it out.

She still hadn't addressed the topic of the perfume on his shirt. And the more she thought about it, the more she realised she had to do it. It was lingering in the back of her mind all the time, and until she brought it into the open, it would stay there, festering like an open wound.

Duncan strode into the living room, her frilly apron tied

around his thick waist. He waved her rolling pin in the air. "Does this go in the dishwasher, love?"

She nodded. "That's fine. Hey, Duncan, can I have a word?"

"Let me put this away. I'll be right with you."

He disappeared back into the kitchen, then re-emerged without the rolling pin or the apron. He sat on the ottoman beside her boot.

"What's up, buttercup?"

She bit down on her lip. How should she broach this subject without sending him into one of his fits? He really did behave like a spoiled toddler at times. And she was rapidly becoming sick of it. Still, she'd prefer to avoid that situation if she could manage it.

"I was doing the laundry a few weeks ago, and I noticed that your shirt smelled like perfume. It wasn't my perfume, but it was strong. And I thought I should ask you about it instead of imagining all kinds of nefarious scenarios in my head." She gave a little laugh to soften her words but watched closely for his reaction.

Duncan's eyes narrowed. "Perfume?"

"That's right. On your work shirt. I found it in your gym bag."

He shook his head. "That can't be right. I don't wear perfume."

"I know that, darling. It was women's perfume."

His cheeks coloured. "You must've imagined it."

"I didn't..." She frowned.

He looked flustered. His gaze darted from the kitchen, back to her face and then the floor.

"I'm sure it was nothing. Maybe I brushed up against someone at work without realising it." He shrugged. "I don't know what to tell you. And I've got to get dinner on or we'll go hungry tonight."

He stalked back into the kitchen and started banging around, opening cabinets and slamming them shut again. She chewed on the end of a pencil, pondering. Was he hiding something from her?

She continued working on the plan for the Surf Club event. There was a meeting tomorrow night with the organising committee, and she needed to have everything ready to show them. She was hoping they could finalise the bulk of the schedule, menu, staffing and music for the event. If they could manage that, she would be able to focus on invitations and marketing efforts.

After a while, Duncan came back into the living room. "Dinner's in the oven. I'm making a roast. But I've got to duck into the office for a bit. Call me if you need anything."

She waved goodbye, wondering what could be so important that he couldn't manage one day away. It was always like that with him. Work came first. She was grateful he'd been such a good provider throughout their marriage. But sometimes she couldn't help feeling jealous of the attention he gave his work and his colleagues. She needed to feel as though she was the centre of his world every now and then. But it'd been a long time since she'd felt that.

Finally, she finished planning and turned the television on. She hadn't watched a movie in a while. It wasn't something she often did. She didn't like to focus for long periods of time. She got twitchy if she sat still too long. But there was nothing else for her to do. She was too tired to go anywhere, and she couldn't walk far. The house was clean. Dinner was in the oven. And Duncan was gone. So, she chose a romantic comedy and settled back in her armchair to enjoy it.

When the phone rang, it jolted her out of her reverie. She'd been so absorbed in the storyline, the ringing had given her a fright. She answered the phone breathlessly.

"Hello?"

"Hi, Mum. It's Brandon. How are you?"

"I'm feeling okay..."

He interrupted her. "Hey, Mum, I was wondering if you could have the two younger kids tomorrow? I'm supposed to watch them, but I've got a few things to do and it would be so much easier to do it all without them. Can I bring them by at nine?"

Irritation burned in her gut. "You want me to watch your two youngest children? Tomorrow?"

"That would be great. Thanks. I'll see you..."

"Wait, Brandon. I didn't say I would."

He hesitated. "Oh... Okay, huh?"

She'd had enough. Her ankle was broken, and he didn't seem to remember that fact, let alone care. "You know I broke my ankle. Right?"

"Oh, yeah. How's that going?"

"It's okay, but I can't run around after two young children. So, no, I can't watch the kids tomorrow. Sorry, honey."

"Just throw on a movie for them. They won't run far," he said with a laugh.

"No, the answer is no, Brandon. You take me for granted. You don't care about how I'm feeling or what I'm going through. And I'm not going to do it this time. You'll have to figure something else out."

The phone went silent.

"Okay, well, have a good evening, honey," she said.

"What's wrong with you, Mum?" he asked, sounding miffed.

"I'm going through some things. And it wouldn't kill you to be a little more supportive of me every now and then."

"What things?" he asked.

"It's personal. But thank you for asking. I appreciate your concern."

"Okay... Well, bye, I guess."

"I'll talk to you later, Brandon. Say hi to the family for me."

When she hung up the phone, she felt strangely elated. She'd finally stood up to one of her children. She felt strong, determined and a little proud of herself. She'd had two confrontations in one day. That had to be some kind of record.

Chapter Twenty-Five

Two weeks later, Emily was folding laundry in the laundry room. She could hear Joanna and Aaron talking in the den. They'd finished dinner and were sitting in front of a muted television while the news played out on the screen.

"How's work going?" Joanna asked.

"It's fine. I'm doing better than I was. It was a steep learning curve, but I think I've got the hang of it now."

"That's good, sweetheart. I'm sure you're doing great. You always were quick to catch on to things. I remember when you were a little boy, your father showed you how to build a model car and from then on, you handled it alone. You were so competent."

"Really? I don't remember that."

"Hmm... Well, it's just one of those things that's stuck out in my mind."

"The commute is killing me, though," he said. "It's over an hour and half without traffic. At peak hour, it's horrendous."

"I'm sorry. That must be hard."

"I'll have to move closer to the office at some point, I guess."

"Don't they have a train?"

"I think there's one, but I'd have to drive there."

"Might be worth looking into," Joanna said. "I'd hate for you to leave just yet. You could stay here a while longer. You're not causing me any trouble, and I love having you here. Besides, it'll give you a chance to save a deposit to buy something of your own. Everything's so expensive these days."

"You're right about that," he replied. "I love living in Sunshine. I can go surfing when I get home, if it's not too late. And on weekends. It's pretty great living by the beach. Maybe I'll hold on for a bit longer. I would like to buy a place of my own. I have some money saved, but it would be good to build up a safety net. That is, if you're okay with me staying a bit longer."

"I'm delighted for you to stay. It's wonderful having Emily here, but I don't know how long she'll stick with me. She's young and has so much potential. And besides, I'm doing so much better these days, I won't need a full-time carer forever. Although I hate to give her up. Still, it would be unfair of me to keep her here. She should be spreading her wings, not fussing around me. And when she goes, I'll be all alone. So, you stay as long as you like, my boy. You living here has been good for me. I didn't realise how much I missed my family."

There was silence. Then the noise of the television burst to life. Emily continued folding clothes while she considered Joanna's words. She hadn't realised Joanna was ready for her to move on. The idea of leaving wasn't something she entertained often. She'd be lying if she said she never thought about it, but she usually dismissed it quickly, since the work was easy and she was paid better than she would be anywhere else with no qualifications or experience to her name. She had room and board, plus a generous stipend. It made life simple. And she was close to her sister.

But there was something to what Joanna said. Lately, Emily had begun to feel a little agitated—like she needed more for her life. She wanted an adventure. Some kind of purpose. A direction to take. And at the moment, she had none of that. Wanda's illness was in the past. Joanna was on the mend. But the idea of leaving, striking out on her own and starting afresh, made nerves jangle in the pit of her stomach.

She was glad Joanna had talked Aaron into staying.

The laundry door opened, and he walked in. "Oh, sorry. I didn't realise you were in here. Is the dryer finished?"

She nodded. "I folded your things and put them on your bed."

"Thanks. You didn't have to do that."

"I don't mind," she said. "It keeps me busy."

"Did you overhear...?" He suddenly looked panicked.

She smiled. "I heard, and it's okay. Jo and I talk about my future sometimes. I know how she feels. She wants the best for me. And I love her for it. But I'm not sure what that is just yet."

He leaned against the washing machine and crossed his ankles. "When we were kids, you wanted to be a ballerina."

She laughed. "Yes, well, I think that ship has officially sailed."

"Do you still dance?"

"Not really. I miss it, though."

"You should start it up again. It takes a lot of discipline to be as good as you were. Don't give that up."

"Maybe. I can't believe you remember that. You never saw me dance."

He smiled. "I watched many of your dances."

"You did? When?"

"Tristan and I may or may not have snuck into dance practice more than once."

"What?" She laughed. "That does surprise me. Tristan always acted like it was a form of torture to go to my recitals."

"He had a crush on Jewel."

"Oh, yeah, that's right. I remember. He was so smitten."

"And she was in your dance group. Plus, I wanted to see you..."

Her breath caught in her throat at the look in his eyes. He stepped closer. She cleared her throat and focused her attention on the shirt she was folding.

"You were always up to something back then."

He folded his arms. "I had a lot of energy and plenty of teenaged angst."

"You filled the principal's car with whipped cream. It smelled so bad, he had to sell it."

"I can't confirm or deny..." He winked.

"And you wanted to see me dance?"

"I was a complicated boy. But I've changed."

"I can see that," she said. "You seem different."

"I've been through some things," he said. "Grown up a bit. Not too much, I hope."

She finished folding and put her hands on either side of the clothes basket. He was in her way. She couldn't get out of the laundry room without pushing past him. She waited.

"Would you have dinner with me?" he asked suddenly.

She frowned. "We eat dinner together every night."

"I mean a date. Would you go on a date with me? Friday night?"

Her heart skipped a beat. "This Friday? Okay."

He smiled and stepped out of the laundry room. "Great. I'm looking forward to it."

Chapter Twenty-Six

Joanna was gardening. She hadn't done it in a while, her knees were already sore. But she'd purchase a special little cushion to kneel on, and it was helping. She dug up a weed and tossed it into the pile. Her gloves were covered in dirt, and it felt good to be out in the late-afternoon air.

The heat of the day had passed. The cool breeze coming in off the water was refreshing. And there were birds swooping and chirping throughout her garden. It was a beautiful day, and she was in a fine mood. Her head was a little dizzy, and there was a feeling in her gut that she should go back inside. But she was ignoring it for now.

"Good afternoon," Chris said.

He stopped at the end of her driveway and smiled at her. He wore a pair of shorts and a collared shirt, with a cap that covered his grey hair and made it poke out in curls in the back. The look suited him.

"Hi there," she said, getting to her feet. She brushed the dirt off her gloves, then pulled them off and laid them in the grass. "Going for a walk?"

He nodded. "It's the perfect time of day for it. Care to join me?"

She glanced at the house. She wanted to go back inside. But his invitation was tempting. Could she manage a walk on the beach? It was what she'd hoped for. She'd longed to feel well enough to do it for years. And she was doing so much better. Maybe the time was right.

"I suppose I could give it a try." She walked to the end of the driveway. Her stomach formed into a knot as she stepped out onto the footpath.

"We can come back anytime you like," he said, and he fell into step beside her.

They walked side by side in silence for a while. Then they crossed the road to get to the beach. She slipped her shoes off at the beach entrance, and they trudged through the soft sand and between the dunes, down to the hard-packed damp sand by the water's edge. All the while, she fought her anxiety to keep it at bay.

Chris was quiet; he seemed deep in thought. Every now and then, he glanced her way.

"Do you mind if I ask you a personal question?" he asked.

"Okay."

"Do you know why it's so hard for you to go outside? When we spoke about it a few weeks back, you mentioned that the loss of your husband and the restaurant were hard for you. But I suppose I was curious to find a connection. It's not my business, though, so it's fine if you'd rather not answer."

She inhaled a slow breath. "It's called agoraphobia. It's been pretty terrible now for about ten years, but lately I've been improving. I'm in therapy, and I think having Aaron move in has helped as well."

"I've noticed you seem to be tackling more outings."

"You know I lost my husband, but what I only hinted at previously is that without him, the restaurant wasn't going to make it. I was a chef, not a manager. I couldn't cope with managing the staff, the books, the suppliers. I'd always had Ron to take care of those things. He was the businessperson, and I was the creative one."

"I can see that. He was a good guy. We knew each other from school. And of course, we were both members of the Rotary Club."

"That's right. I remember those meetings. He loved all of that. And you're right, he was the best," Joanna replied, recalling him fondly.

She didn't get upset when she talked about him anymore. But for years, she hadn't been able to say his name without bursting into tears. "He was my rock. And honestly, the only reason I enjoyed working at the restaurant and cooking was for him. When we had children, I didn't work at the restaurant nearly as much. He hired another chef, and I filled in when he needed me to. But then the children grew up, and I went back to full-time. We were a great team. I loved the restaurant, the food, the people, being with Ron all day every day. It was the best time of my life."

"It's a real blessing to have that kind of marriage and partnership," Chris said.

A flock of seagulls lifted into the air around them, cawing as they rose on the breeze.

"I was very blessed. But then he died, all of a sudden. I wasn't expecting it and hadn't prepared myself for the possibility. After all, he was only mid-fifties. I couldn't believe it. We were so young. And then he was gone. The restaurant became a huge stone around my neck—I couldn't go anywhere or do anything other than run the place. It took up every waking moment. And before long, it was losing money. A lot of money."

Waves crashed to shore. The hushing of the water as it

frothed close to their feet was comforting. She felt her anxiety fading.

"I was worried I would lose the place. I started looking for buyers. And then there was a fire. I was at the restaurant late at night, alone. I fell asleep at my desk in a pile of paperwork, and sometime during the night, the smoke set off the alarms. I woke up, completely disoriented and confused."

"Wow, that's horrible."

"It was. I was so scared. I tried to get out of my office, but a beam fell to the ground and pinned me down. I could feel and see the entire restaurant burning down around me. The smoke was so thick. I panicked. I couldn't get out, and yet I knew if I didn't that I'd die."

"I had no idea. I knew there'd been a fire, but I didn't realise you were in it. I was away at the time, visiting family."

"I don't talk about it much. Anyway, someone called the fire department, and they pulled me out of there. I was in the hospital for weeks. Karen did her best but she was busy with her own family. Gwen and Debbie were so great—they cared for me. But when I was back at home and I'd fully recovered, they all went back to living their lives, and that's when the nightmares started. At first, I didn't really go anywhere because I wasn't well enough, but after a while, it was because I didn't want to, and then it became almost impossible. I'd have panic attacks and flashbacks."

"I'm sorry that happened. You must've been really traumatised by it."

"Some people would've managed it better, I know. And I used to beat myself up about that. But I've come to accept it. This is how my mind coped with the trauma of losing Ron and the fire. And after that, the legal issues with the insurance company who claimed I'd set fire to the restaurant because it was in financial trouble." She sighed. "I didn't open up about it with anyone for a while. Karen didn't realise I was going through all of that and she moved away. But hiding it only made it worse for me."

"That's a lot for anyone to deal with," he said.

"Thank you. I'm so grateful for all the help I've received, and Emily has truly been a godsend. She's helped so much in recent years. And it's made all the difference in my recovery. I really believe that."

"You didn't give up on yourself or on getting better. I think that's been a big part of it too," he said. "And look at you now — taking a walk on the beach. I think you should be proud of yourself."

"I am," she said. "Thank you for encouraging me to join you. It's a big step for me."

"How is Emily?" Chris asked. "Is she coping with having Aaron live there?"

Joanna smiled. "I think she's enjoying it as much as I am."

"Oh, really?" He grinned. "They would make a good match."

"I think so too. Although I hate it when things change. I think the two of them would be very good for one another. I love my grandson, and he couldn't find a nicer, sweeter girl than Emily. She's a beautiful soul and never has a cross word for anyone."

"If that's true, then I hope they can make it work. Because there's nothing better in all the world than finding that person who makes your heart sing."

Joanna laughed. "Christopher Hampton, I had no idea you were such a romantic and a poet!"

He winked. "There's a lot you don't know about me."

"Colour me intrigued."

"I guess you'll just have to find out the old-fashioned way."

Joanna dipped her head to hide her smile. She was flirting, and she thought perhaps he was as well. It'd been a long time since she'd had any inclination to do that. And it felt good.

Chapter Twenty-Seven

Gwen hobbled across Joanna's den and sat on the couch with a grunt. "This boot is really quite annoying."

Joanna set a glass of pinot noir down in front of her. "I'll bet it is. Let's hope they can remove it soon."

"Three more weeks," Gwen said as she picked up the wine glass.

"You can do it," Debbie replied. She sipped at the wine in her hand. "Three weeks will fly by."

"I'm grateful at least that it's not plaster like in the good old days."

"That is a blessing," Joanna replied with a nod. "And how are things going with Duncan?"

Gwen didn't know how to answer that. Her friends would be disappointed that she hadn't pushed harder about the perfume on the shirt, or that she hadn't looked through his phone. But that just wasn't her. She wasn't comfortable with confrontation or with snooping.

"I suppose it's all fine. He's been helping out a little more around the house. Although I doubt it will last."

"And did you find anything in his emails?" Debbie asked.

"I haven't looked. Honestly, I can't imagine he'd be unfaithful."

"Are you sure?"

"No, I'm not sure. We don't spend much time together. We haven't been intimate in years. He doesn't seem particularly interested in me anymore, other than as his companion and housekeeper."

"How romantic," Joanna said in a dry tone.

"Where is he now?" Debbie asked.

"He's at work—he'll probably be on his way to the gym shortly. He goes right after work. Then sometimes he has a drink with friends and comes home at around seven for dinner."

"It sounds like he has a healthy social life," Joanna said.

"But without including you, his wife," Debbie added.

"I've asked if I could go to the gym with him, but he says it's his alone time."

"And you fell for that?" Joanna said.

"You're feeling feisty today, I see," Gwen replied with a roll of the eyes. "Yes, I took him at his word. If he needs alone time, I'm not going to stop him."

"But how much alone time can one man need? It seems selfish to me. You're at home all the time, taking care of your children and now grandchildren. You don't get out much. But he needs time to himself after work, and then with friends, but not with you? That sounds fishy to me," Debbie stated. "I think you should surprise him at the gym. Get on your workout gear and show up to exercise with him. It might be romantic."

"Or it could be a disaster," Joanna added.

"That too," Debbie agreed.

"But at least I'd know if he wanted me around or not, I suppose," Gwen replied. "I can't exactly work out, given the state of my ankle. But I could show up at the gym to spend time with him. Maybe take him out for a drink myself instead of him waiting to go with friends after his workout."

"I think it's a great idea," Debbie said. "If you want things to change in your relationship, you've got to change the cycle. That's what I did. I stayed home, made dinner and forced my husband to talk to me about what was wrong."

"And did he?" Joanna asked.

"He did. It was hard and emotional. He shared that he's struggled ever since the miscarriage."

"Boy! That was a long time ago," Gwen said. "But I can understand that must've been hard for him. For both of you."

"We should've talked about it together," Debbie said. "But we were both hurting and trying to be strong for the other one, and we brushed it under the rug."

"You're talking now, and that's what matters," Joanna said.

"Yes, it is," Debbie agreed. "And I think that's what you should do with Duncan. Show up at the gym, whisk him away for drinks, change the cycle of behaviour you've gotten into. You're in a rut. You need to get some romance and connection back in your relationship."

"I can't believe you made us come with you," Joanna grumbled as she held on to the car door. Gwen knew Joanna got carsick, but she didn't have time to think about that right now. She had more important things to focus on, like the fact that her boot kept knocking into the brake pedal.

"You didn't have to come," Gwen countered as she steered her car around a roundabout. "You said you didn't want to miss out."

"Are you supposed to be driving with a broken ankle?" Debbie asked.

"It's fine," Gwen said. "It's my left foot that's the issue. My right foot is perfect."

Gwen was feeling nervous. What would Duncan say? She'd asked Debbie and Joanna to accompany her to the gym because she had a feeling Duncan would tell her he wanted to finish his workout and go home, and that she was being silly for suggesting anything else. And if he did that, she needed her friends with her so she could laugh it off and go do something fun together. If they weren't there, she would sit in her car and cry while thinking about how she didn't know what to do to save her marriage.

There was a lot riding on this.

"You know, if he's not there, or he doesn't want to go out with you, we'll just grab some drinks together. I saw this really great place nearby that I've been meaning to try out, but I've just been too busy," Debbie said. "This is the perfect time to do that."

Gwen slowed as the car neared the gym. "Hmmm... Okay." She was looking about the car park frantically, hoping to spot Duncan's BMW. If it was parked, that meant he was already working out and she'd have to wait. That would be a relief, really. She and her friends could grab a drink, and then she could catch her husband on his way home.

"Do you see his car?" Joanna asked, craning her neck to look around Debbie's seat.

Gwen shook her head. "It's pretty early. He may not be here yet." She pulled into a parking space and switched off the car. "We can wait a little while. He loves a strict routine, so he shouldn't be long."

She turned on the radio. Whitney Houston's *"I Wanna Dance with Somebody"* came on. "Oh, I love this song." Gwen started to sing along to the lyrics. And soon all three of them were shouting out the words at the top of their lungs as they bopped about in their seats.

This was one of the things Gwen adored about her friends. When things were tough, they were always there for her and knew exactly what she needed. They could be silly and sing together like they were teenagers all over again, and it filled her heart. Beneath the surface, an understanding loomed —her marriage was in trouble. It was a realisation she'd been avoiding for too long.

The front doors of the gym were glass. She could see some of the workout equipment in the background. A young woman stood outside the doors wearing yoga pants, a crop top and a bag slung over one shoulder. She played with her phone, hair slipping forward to partially obscure her face.

The song came to an end, and Gwen turned down the radio. "We should go. I don't know what I was thinking. If Duncan sees me here, he'll think I've lost my mind."

"Maybe that's a good thing," Joanna suggested. "It might make him realise it's time for a change."

Gwen glanced in her rearview mirror and noticed a black BMW pull into a parking space behind them. Duncan climbed out of the driver's side door with a black backpack. He wore a buttoned shirt, a tie and a pair of navy slacks. He must've seen her because he waved in her direction and then jogged across the road towards her car. She was about to open the door to greet him when he ran right by and onto the footpath.

The woman in the yoga pants glanced up at him and smiled. Gwen's heart froze. Yoga Pants Woman put her phone in a pocket and reached up her arms to encircle Duncan's neck. His own hands slipped around her slim waist. He leaned in and kissed her on the mouth.

"Is that Duncan?" Debbie asked from the passenger seat.

Gwen couldn't answer. Her voice caught in her throat.

Joanna leaned forward. "Is he kissing that woman?"

"Oh, no," Debbie whispered.

Gwen didn't move. Her throat was so painful, it felt as though a rock was lodged in it. She wanted to scream, to cry, to do something. Instead, she pulled her phone out of her purse and snapped a photo of her husband kissing a stranger.

"What are you doing?" Joanna asked, aghast.

"I'm going to show this to him, and then we can finally have a real conversation," Gwen said. She was amazed at how calm she sounded. She didn't feel that way on the inside. Inside, she was wailing and beating her fists against the walls that surrounded her.

"Are you going to say something to him now?" Debbie asked gently.

Gwen shook her head. She watched as Duncan and the woman walked into the gym through the automatic glass doors. "No, I'll speak to him at home. There's no point making a scene. I don't have the strength for it."

They drove back to Joanna's house, where Gwen dropped her and Debbie at the curb. She couldn't bring herself to go inside.

"Come in for a drink, honey," Joanna said. "I have a divine chocolate torte I made as well. It'll do the trick."

"No, thanks, Jo. I need to be alone," she replied.

As she drove away, she could see Debbie and Joanna watching her in the rearview mirror. They looked worried. She turned her attention to the road, and her fingers clenched around the steering wheel. What would she do? Duncan was having an affair. She'd suspected it for a while but hadn't really believed it was true. Being faced with the evidence had taken her breath away. He'd been her world for so long, she couldn't remember who she was before he came along. There was no clear way forward. She wished she didn't know. It was better when she was ignorant and naive, living in her big house and watching the grandkids every other day, completely ignorant of the fact that her life was a lie.

She pulled her car into the garage and sat still while the door whirred shut. Then she hobbled into the house and collapsed into her bed. She pulled the covers up to her chin, curled onto her side and cried.

Chapter Twenty-Eight

After half an hour, Gwen's tears dried up. She still didn't move, though. She wasn't sure what to do next. Usually at this time of day, she'd be making Duncan's dinner. But she wasn't about to do that now. And she wasn't hungry. So instead, she simply lay still in her bed staring at the clock on the bedside table as the minutes ticked by. Every minute that passed brought the confrontation closer.

The doorbell rang, and her heart lurched as though she was being attacked. Her nerves were frayed. She swung her feet over the edge of the bed and made her way to the door, straightening her hair and clothes as she went.

When the door swung open, Debbie and Joanna were standing there. Joanna raised a casserole dish in the air, and Debbie lifted a bottle of wine high over her head.

"We've brought supplies. You shouldn't be alone right now," Joanna said in her calm, sympathetic way.

"Plus, you'll need wine," Debbie added.

"You two are amazing," Gwen replied as she shuffled forward to embrace them both at once. "Come on in. I'll find glasses."

"I made chicken and dumplings. It's one of my favourite comfort foods," Joanna said. "As soon as it was done, we hurried over. It's still burning hot."

"That's so thoughtful. I wasn't going to eat dinner, but now I will. Thank you."

"We figured Duncan wouldn't be home yet, so we could drop by for a quick visit to give you some support." Joanna set the casserole dish on the kitchen bench. "And I don't know how you're feeling, but your house looks fantastic."

Gwen chuckled. "Thank you. I haven't watched the kiddos for a while, so it's staying clean, which is nothing short of a miracle."

"Whatever you're doing, it's working."

"I miss them, though," Gwen said. "I didn't realise how much I would miss them. But it's been weeks since I've really spent any time with them. I've visited, and they've popped by, but it's not the same as when they stay all day. And their smiling little faces mean so much to me."

"You needed a break," Joanna said, then grimaced. "No pun intended."

They all laughed.

"I needed a break, so my body gave it to me," Gwen replied, her eyes glistening with tears of laughter.

"But that doesn't mean you don't love spending time with the kids. It's just that maybe you should have them for shorter periods or not quite so often." Debbie opened the bottle of wine, then searched the cupboards until she found glasses.

"We *are* getting older," Joanna agreed. "I know we don't like to admit that."

"Hush your mouth," Debbie said as she filled each glass with red wine. "None of that talk."

"I suppose you're right," Gwen said. "I should be slowing down. At least a little bit."

"They won't be young forever," Joanna added. "My

grandkids are mostly grown now. I miss them being small. And I wish they lived closer."

"I know," Gwen said with a shake of her head. "They wear me out, but I really wouldn't change it for anything. I should be grateful, not complaining. And now look what's happened —I complained about my husband, and he's..." She couldn't finish her sentence. A lump grew in her throat.

"Here you go," Debbie said gently as she handed Gwen a glass. "Take a sip, and then we can talk about what comes next."

Gwen gulped down a mouthful of wine. "What should I do? What would you do?" She searched Debbie's face, then Joanna's.

Joanna offered her a rueful smile. "It's been so long since I was married..."

Gwen reached out to squeeze her arm. "I'm sorry, honey."

"It's okay. But honestly, if Ron were here right now, I wouldn't care about anything else other than seeing him again."

"I know that's true," Gwen replied, tears blurring her vision. Joanna had loved her husband so much. It was one of the saddest experiences of her life having to help her friend through the trauma of losing him.

"I would leave him," Debbie said bluntly. "I'm sorry, but if he cheated on me that way, I would have to leave. I couldn't possibly trust him again. I know some people are fine with giving second chances, and generally I would agree. But not for something like this. Not me."

Gwen sighed. "I feel the same way. I want to forgive him and forget. I truly do. But I know deep down that this is his way of telling me the marriage is over. If I forgave him, he'd only keep doing it. And he'd lose respect for me as well. I can't see how that would work."

"You should talk to him," Joanna said. "See what he has to say."

"Or you could throw all his things out onto the driveway," Debbie added with a twinkle in her eye. She drained her wine glass. "Let him find out the hard way that you know."

"I don't think that's the best approach..." Joanna began.

"But she's right," Gwen interrupted. "You know what Duncan's like. As soon as I raise the subject, he'll pretend I'm making up the whole thing. Then when I show him the photo, he'll yell and rage and make it all my fault. And then before I know it, I'm the bad guy and he's forgiven and everything will keep going the way it always has."

"You're too easy on him," Debbie agreed.

"You're married," Joanna said. "You should talk about it like two mature adults."

"I don't want him in the house," Gwen said, steeling her nerves with another gulp of wine. "Debbie has the right idea —I'm going to throw his things onto the driveway, like a symbolic act."

"What will that do other than make him angry?" Joanna asked.

"We have smart locks on every door. I can change the code and then lock him out of the system," Gwen said, her heart racing. She could actually do this. She could keep him from the house. It was reckless and crazy, but suddenly it was all she wanted to do.

"Really? Lock him out?" Joanna's eyes widened. "I don't know..."

"It's perfect," Debbie exclaimed with a laugh. "We need to move quickly. Either you're in or you're out, Gilston. Which is it?"

Joanna rolled her eyes. "You two will be the death of me. Okay, I'm in. But I'm putting a disclaimer on this right now— I advised against it."

"Yes, Your Honour," Debbie replied as she gave a mock bow. "Now, let's do it."

* * *

It only took them half an hour to throw a few of Duncan's things into a suitcase and then set it out on the driveway. Gwen decided against throwing things willy-nilly, since it made her inner neat freak uncomfortable. She'd even packed his toiletry kit with everything he'd need to stay in a hotel, along with several of his favourite business suits. He would be going to work each day and would need things to wear. She didn't want him to be humiliated.

Then she went into the office and worked on the security system. She'd had it installed a year earlier when the kids were coming and going so much. Instead of handing out keys, which they often lost, she decided on a code system. And they'd replaced all the locks with smart ones. She changed the codes so none of Duncan's would work. He could get into the garage with his clicker but wouldn't be able to get inside the house. She also changed the login for the security system.

Then they all went to the sitting room at the front of the house to wait, and they opened another bottle of wine. They were just finishing up their second bottle when the garage door opened. It was dark outside, and the external lights had come on, illuminating the garden path and garage door.

The suitcase was placed directly in front of the car space that Duncan used, so he wouldn't be able to miss it or go around it. Gwen's heart thudded against her ribcage as she heard Duncan's car stop, then the car door open.

They hurried to look out the front window. He was standing, staring down at the suitcase with his headlights flooding the entire driveway. He reached for the suitcase and wheeled it back into the garage, then got into his car and drove it inside.

Gwen, Debbie, and Joanna then moved as quickly as Gwen could manage to the inner door to the garage and listened closely.

The door handle jiggled. There was a beeping sound, a curse and another jiggle.

"Gwen! Open up. Something's wrong with the door."

Gwen inhaled a quick breath. "I changed the code."

"What? Huh? I didn't hear you. Can you open it?"

She braced herself. "I changed the code!"

Her phone rang. It was Duncan. She answered it. "Hello, Duncan."

He hesitated. "Gwen, what's going on? The door to the garage isn't working. And there was a suitcase in the driveway."

Gwen moved into the living room and sat in her armchair with a sigh. "I saw you, Duncan. I saw you kiss that woman at the gym."

He didn't reply for several seconds. "What?"

"You kissed her. Don't pretend you didn't."

"Open the door, Gwenny. We need to talk in person."

"Not today, Duncan. I can't face you right now. I need some time. I packed you a bag. You can go stay with your new friend for all I care." She sighed. "I don't want you in my house."

"Our house, Gwen." His voice grew louder. "It's our house, and I have every right to be inside right now. You can't lock me out of my own house!"

"I want to talk to you about all of it, but not today. We can touch base again soon, when you're calm." He always hated when she told him to calm down, but this time, he had no bargaining chip.

"It's not what you thought. You saw something and misinterpreted it. I can explain if you'll just open the door."

"I know what I saw," she replied. "I have a photo of the two of you kissing. Who is she? Do you love her?"

"It doesn't matter who she is, just someone I met at work. And no, I don't love her. I love you. You're my wife. You can't lock me out of your life like this."

"We can talk tomorrow, Duncan."

"No, wait!"

She hung up the phone and stared at it blankly. Debbie leaned down to give her a hug.

"I know that was hard," Joanna said.

"I feel strangely unemotional right now," Gwen replied. "I'm sure it will hit me later."

Duncan's car started up again and reversed out of the garage. The door closed behind him, and he accelerated down the driveway then turned onto the road.

"Let's have some dinner and watch a movie," Joanna suggested.

"That's a great idea," Debbie said.

"Okay," Gwen agreed. "But please don't make me choose. I don't think I could."

"Not a problem. I've been wanting a good cry myself lately, so I'm thinking *Steel Magnolias*."

"That sounds perfect," Gwen said. "Let's go into the theatre. Duncan had it built so he could watch football with his friends. But he's hardly ever used it."

"Chicken and dumplings coming right up," Joanna said.

Chapter Twenty-Nine

Emily stared at the large container of chicken and dumplings in the fridge. It looked as though Joanna had made dinner, but she was nowhere to be found. Emily had spent the afternoon with her sister. When she got home, the house was dark and Joanna wasn't home.

She wasn't accustomed to finding Joanna gone. She hadn't done that in the entire time Emily had known her. Simply vanished without any kind of warning. She tried calling her, but the phone kept going directly to voicemail. Hopefully she was okay and nothing bad had happened. The car was still in the garage, so she couldn't have gone far. Unless she'd driven with someone else.

It was really very confusing.

She wandered around the house for a while, hoping that Joanna would call. Then finally, her hunger pangs drove her back to the kitchen. She piled a bowl full of chicken and dumplings to reheat. Then she filled a glass with Chardonnay and headed to the den.

Since she was home alone, she might as well eat in front of the television. She'd been watching a new show about a celebrity traveling around Italy and eating the food in every city and town. She'd missed the past few weeks. This would give her a chance to catch up. And she wouldn't be ravenous as she usually was, since she had dinner in front of her.

With the show primed and ready to go, she sat in her favourite love seat and ate dinner while watching. It was nice to have a little time to herself. Halfway through the show, Joanna finally texted that she was fine and out with Debbie and Gwen. That helped Emily relax.

Then the front door slammed. She heard footsteps, and Aaron's head poked around the doorway. "There you are."

"Hi," she said. "Hungry?"

"Starved."

"There's chicken and dumplings in the fridge."

"Perfect," he replied. "I love Gran's chicken and dumplings. She makes it so delicious."

He soon returned with a bowl and sat on the same couch. She wriggled over a little to make room for him.

"What are we watching?" he asked.

"A show about food."

"We're going to watch a show about food while eating food?" He laughed.

She grinned. "Of course. My philosophy is that you can't have too much of a good thing."

"After dinner, I'm going to test out this theory on the chocolate cake I saw in the fridge."

"How was work?"

"It was fine. There's a guy in my team who's always trying to get me in trouble. Blames me for everything, but not openly. You know? He's passive-aggressive with it. Today he told the boss he was sorry we couldn't make the deadline for this iteration since I've been struggling with the code."

"Wow. What did you say?"

"There's not much I can say. I'm not struggling with the

code. But how do I say that in a meeting when he's been at the company longer than me? Should I tell them he's lying? I don't think that would go over well."

"I'm sure they know what he's like."

"That's probably true." His shoulder bumped up against hers. He glanced at her, and their eyes met. "Where's Gran?"

"Out with her friends."

His eyes widened. "I wasn't expecting you to say that. Good for her. She's doing so well lately."

"I'm proud of her," Emily replied.

"I don't want to speak out of turn, but does that change your position...?"

She shrugged. "I don't know. But probably."

"Have you thought any more about what you want to do?"

"I'm considering going to uni. When I left school, I wasn't ready to dive right back into studying. And besides, I wasn't sure what I should study. But now, I feel like it might be the right time."

"What would you study?"

"I was looking at the website last night for the Sunshine Coast University. They have a midwifery course there that looks interesting."

"Babies?" he asked.

She nodded. "I've always loved taking care of people, but especially babies. I think it would be so exciting to help them come into the world."

"That's a great idea. You'd be perfect at that. You're so kind and gentle."

Her cheeks flushed with warmth. "Thanks."

His shoulder pressed against hers again, and this time, it was as though a bolt of electricity passed between them. His encouragement meant so much to her. Sometimes it felt as though no one really saw who she was. But he did.

Chapter Thirty

The next day, Joanna woke up with her first hangover in decades. She held her head as she swung her feet out of bed. Then with a groan, she stood.

"I shouldn't have had that last glass of wine," she grumbled as she wandered to the shower.

She showered and dressed, then padded out to the kitchen in her slippers to find some paracetamol. Emily sat at the dining table with a laptop open in front of her. She glanced up with a smile.

"Good morning. Although, the morning is almost over. You must've been out late."

Joanna groaned. "I need coffee and Panadol. Reverse the order."

Emily laughed as she got to her feet. "Take a seat. I'll get it for you. Are you hung over?"

Joanna sat at the table and dropped her head in her hands.

"I don't think I've ever seen you like this. What on earth did you ladies get up to last night?" Emily filled a glass with water and brought Joanna two capsules.

She swallowed them with a gulp. Then she took another swig of water. "Duncan is having an affair."

"Oh, no. She's sure?"

Joanna nodded. "We saw him."

"Poor Gwen."

"So, we stayed with her, ate and drank, and watched a movie. It was fun, but we're sad for her, of course. I shouldn't have had so much wine, though. I don't usually drink more than a small glass. And now I'm paying for it." She grunted.

"It was all for a good cause. I'll make you some breakfast."

"No bacon, please. I don't think I could swallow it."

"Eggs?"

"Yes, thanks."

While Emily was cooking, Joanna's phone rang. She picked it up and forced a smile onto her face. She found that when she smiled, her voice sounded more friendly, and she wasn't feeling friendly. "Hello, this is Jo."

"Joanna, it's Bobbie. How are you?"

"I'm great, Bobbie. How are you? I hope the manuscript looks good."

"It's great. I'm calling to let you know that the initial round of edits are underway and I'll be sending you some notes shortly."

They chatted a little more about the book and next steps. Then Joanna hung up the phone. "We'll be getting some initial notes back on the first draft of the manuscript soon. I'll have to set aside some time to focus on it when it comes through."

"Let me know how I can help," Emily said.

Joanna wandered to the office to check her email. When she returned, her eggs were sitting on a piece of toast waiting for her. Fried the way she liked them, with the yolk still runny.

"It's in the inbox, and the comments are positive!" she said, excitement buzzing in her gut and her hangover forgotten. "There's nothing that beats the feeling of finishing a book except perhaps having your editor rave about it."

"I have to say I agree," Emily replied. "This was my first book, and I enjoyed the experience."

"Did you? I'm glad."

"It was a lot more work than I realised it would be, though."

Joanna laughed. "It always is."

After breakfast, there was a knock at the door. When Joanna opened it, Debbie and Gwen were there. Gwen held up a bottle of champagne.

"It's time to celebrate," Debbie said. "We brought champagne! We thought we should celebrate the cookbook. We never really took the time to appreciate what we achieved."

"Oh, wow. Come on in," Joanna said. "I don't think I can drink today, but I appreciate the effort."

"It's non-alcoholic," Gwen replied.

"Perfect," Joanna said.

"Bobbie loves it!" Debbie declared as she set a box of chocolates on the counter. "I assume you all got the email. I'm so proud of us."

"Yes! Me too," Joanna said. "It's something I've always wanted to do. *The Sunshine Potluck Society Cookbook* will be on its way to bookshelves across the world before we know it."

"It's so exciting," Gwen said.

"Are you sure you want to celebrate today?" Joanna asked.

Gwen popped the top of the champagne with a laugh. "Anything to get my mind off my marriage. Yes, please!"

Emily joined them as they each filled a glass. Then they held them high and clinked them together.

"Cheers!" Emily said.

"To our cookbook," Joanna added.

"To our cookbook!" they all agreed.

Chapter Thirty-One

After their champagne celebration, Gwen had an appointment at the hospital to get her ankle checked out. The doctor said it had healed well and she was free to begin walking on it as usual for some part of each day, but that she should continue using the boot for the full six weeks. The appointment was faster than she anticipated, which she was grateful for since she had the Surf Club fundraiser that night.

As she walked back to her car, her leg felt light and free. She would drive home without the boot, then put it on again when she arrived. She couldn't wait to be free of it entirely. She climbed into her car. The rest of the day would be full of party preparations. She had a major event to run. Major for the island and for her, anyway.

She couldn't have added more items to her to-do list for the day if she'd tried.

Back at the house, she put on her boot and steamed her evening dress for the festivities. She'd managed to find a dress that would allow her to run about all evening in a boot while still looking elegant. At least she thought it was elegant. It had a wide skirt and hung off her shoulders. She intended to curl her hair and wear a faux fur around her shoulders. It was the best she could do given the timing and the other distractions in her life. If she made it through the event with her sanity intact, she'd consider that a win.

There was a knock at the front door, and it surprised her. She laid the steamer down on the counter in her bathroom and hurried to answer. Duncan stood there, looking dishevelled and tired.

"I wasn't expecting you," she said.

"We need to talk."

She waved him inside, and they sat in the front room.

He sighed and leaned forward. "You have to let me explain. You're misunderstanding things, and it's not what you think."

She held up a hand. "I'm going to stop you right there because it hurts even more that you'd try to gaslight me."

"Gaslight?" he asked, one eyebrow quirked.

"Yes, I'm hip and I know things." She opened her phone, browsed to the photograph of him with his mistress, and held it up for him to see. "As you can tell, I captured the kiss quite nicely."

He leaned back in his chair, eyes flashing. "What did you expect, Gwen? We haven't connected as a couple in years. You aren't blameless, you know. You've neglected me for so long, I can barely recall anything different."

"Neglected you? I do everything for you."

He shrugged. "I need more than that. We don't talk. We have nothing in common. You have your friends and the grandkids, the occasional fundraiser and books. But I'm not really interested in those things. I was looking for more, and I found it."

She swallowed down the lump in her throat. "I see. So, I sacrifice my own life, wants and needs for this family for decades, and then suddenly that makes me boring and worthless?"

"That's not what I'm saying," he said with a grunt. "Don't twist my words."

"That's what it sounds like to me."

The doorbell rang.

"What on earth? Who could that be?" Gwen was feeling flustered. She still had so much to do before the fundraiser. So many things to organise, and she wasn't dressed yet. Her family and friends all knew about the fundraiser. She'd spoken about it with them several times. Yet here was Duncan, monopolising her time right when she was supposed to be getting ready for the event. And now someone else was at her door as well. Anxiety fluttered in her belly.

"Hey, Mum," Brandon said. He had two children with him. Both had snotty noses. "I have a meeting in ten minutes. Is there any chance you could take the kids for the rest of the day? Of course they both had to get sick when I've got a full schedule. And Mara is in surgery all day long."

Gwen's eyes narrowed. "You're asking me to watch the kids?"

"Yes, please." He smiled. "You're a lifesaver. I'll call you later." He turned to leave.

"Wait!" Gwen shouted. "Do you remember anything about what I've got going on today?"

Brandon's brow furrowed. "Today? Um..."

She crossed her arms. "Brandon Lee Prince, you know I'm organising the Surf Club fundraiser. It's on tonight—I sent you and Mara an invitation weeks ago. I can't watch the kids. I'm getting dressed to leave. And I have an enormous amount of work to do before the event."

"Oh. Can you take the kids with you?"

She wanted to scream. Instead, she drew in a deep, calming

breath. "No, I can't take the kids, honey. I'm going to be very busy. Why don't you ask your father? He's right here. I'm sure he doesn't have anything else to do."

Brandon poked his head through the front door. "Dad?"

Duncan rose to greet him. "Hi, son."

"Do you think you could watch the kids for me?"

Confusion filtered across Duncan's features. "Me? Watch the kids?"

"It would be a big help."

Gwen ushered them both out the front door. She gave Duncan a little shove in the back to get him over the threshold. "That sounds wonderful. The two of you can work things out between you. But he can't watch the kids here, since he doesn't live here anymore. Love you, Bran. Hope it works out. Bye-bye."

She slammed the door shut. She shouldn't have said that bit about him not living there anymore. Or at least phrased it differently. It was callous, since it was the first Brandon was hearing about it. She'd wanted to break it to her children gently. But they weren't kids anymore, and they should be able to process their parents separating. Perhaps she should call them later to discuss it and try to smooth things over a bit. She hated the thought of any of her family being upset with her. But she couldn't dwell on that now. She had a lot to accomplish.

* * *

Later that night, Gwen stood off to the side of the silent auction with a forced smile on her face. She was exhausted. Her feet ached, her back was in spasms, and she had some kind of cramp in her side. But the entire evening so far had been a huge success.

Debbie and Caleb were moving slowly around the nearby

dance floor like a pair of movie stars. She couldn't help feeling a little jealous. The way Caleb held his wife in his arms was inspiring. If only she and Duncan could have half of the love those two shared. She was so happy they'd been able to work things out between them. They looked like two teenagers in love all over again.

Debbie wore her hair teased high with a very impressive low cut dress. It had a wide skirt and lace around the hem. Joanna was in something similar although not quite so pouffy. And her makeup was more subtle. But both of them had made a big effort to dress for the theme.

Brandon spotted her from across the room. He and Mara made their way over to her. Brandon was in a black and white three-piece suit. Mara wore a long sparkling gown with a bustle. Brandon pushed his hands into his pockets and cleared his throat.

"Mum, when you said that Dad didn't live with you anymore..."

She'd been expecting this question. She'd hoped that Duncan would've explained things to their son, but of course he'd leave that up to her, like he did everything.

"He's moved out, honey. I'm sorry, I know that's probably upsetting to you. But we're separated."

Brandon's face paled. "I can't believe it. Why? What happened?"

She sighed. "This isn't the time or place for this conversation. I have to go and pay the caterer, and my friends want me to join them on the dance floor. There's a lot going on, honey. I want to talk to you about it, but not right now."

She hugged him and Mara goodbye, then hurried into the kitchen to pay the caterer. Afterwards, she wandered back out to the dance floor to see if Debbie and Caleb had hung around. Most of the guests had already gone home, but

Debbie and Caleb were sipping cocktails on two stools at the bar. Gwen went to join them.

She sat down with a groan as the pain suddenly subsided. "My poor feet."

Debbie smiled at her. "You did an amazing job, Gwen. The entire night was perfect."

"You think so?"

"Yes, we bid on a day trip around the Whitsundays on a yacht. I'm so excited. I hope we win."

Caleb laughed. "I'll take you on a day trip even if we don't."

Debbie leaned into his chest. "That would be wonderful."

Gwen watched them and felt her throat tighten. "You two give me hope. You know that?"

"Maybe you and Duncan can work things out," Debbie suggested.

"No, I don't think so," Gwen replied. "We talked, and he's still unrepentant. Blames me for it all."

"I'm so sorry, sweetie."

"It's okay. Time for a new season. The whole world is open to me now. I've been waiting to travel with Duncan when he took some time off work or retired. But now I can go anywhere I like, whenever I want to go. It'll be lonely, but I'll get used to it." She lifted her chin. "I'm sure I'll have a great time."

"Well, I'm going to the loo, then we should leave," Caleb said, rising to his feet. "It was a great party, Gwen. Well done."

"Thanks, Caleb."

When he'd left, Gwen leaned forward to whisper to Debbie, "You two look very cozy."

Debbie laughed. "I know. It's like everything between us opened up when he finally shared with me how he felt. He'd been holding all this stuff inside for so long, it'd eaten away at him. I know there'll be more for us to deal with, and we agreed that Friday nights will be a date night where we share what's on our hearts. We don't ever want to get back to that place where we feel so disconnected from each other. And the romance is more than just words, let me just say that." Debbie's cheeks flushed pink.

Gwen laughed. "'More Than Words.' That's one of my favourite songs."

"I know," Debbie replied with a wink. "Mine too."

Chapter Thirty-Two

The office was buzzing when Debbie went in the next day. It felt good to be back, although she was tired and her head was pounding from the fundraiser the night before. Who thought it would be a good idea to put the event on a Thursday night? She'd have to make that point to Gwen the next time she saw her.

Her inbox was a disaster area. There were hundreds of unread emails. She worked her way through them slowly, stopping for client meetings and the weekly staff meeting.

She was pleasantly surprised to find that there had been no emergencies this time when she was out of the office. And the team had managed to figure out how to deal with every issue that arose, simply copying her in on email threads so she could catch up.

By lunchtime, she was feeling better. She went out to lunch with the partners so they could update her on each of their clients and the status of each active case. There was a divorce that was particularly messy, but it was being handled professionally by the team. Another case involved a lawsuit for a real estate investment gone wrong. The litigation team was at full capacity and bringing in more than their budgeted billable hours, which was good to see.

After a lunch of grilled barramundi and steamed vegetables with a side of brown rice, she went back to the office to finish her work for the day. She was determined to get home earlier than she normally would, and with her reduced workload, after having handed many of her most time-consuming clients over to the rest of the team, it looked as though she would manage it.

Her desk phone rang, and she answered while typing out an email. "Hello. Debbie Holmes speaking."

"Debbie Holmes, this is Caleb Holmes." Her husband's voice sent a thrill up her spine, and she smiled.

"Why are you calling my desk phone?"

"I called your mobile. You didn't answer."

She reached into her purse and pulled out the mobile. "Oh, sorry. I have it on silent."

"Well, I wanted to see if you would go on a date with me tonight."

"A date?" She grinned and leaned back in her chair. "That sounds nice. Where are we going?"

"It's a surprise. But it will involve food."

"Good, because I love food."

"I know you do."

"It's my love language."

"Lucky for me," he replied with a chuckle.

"No hints?"

"Not one. But do you think you could get home a little early?"

"Already planning on it," she said. "I'll see you around five."

"That would be perfect," he said. "See you then. Love you."

After she hung up the phone, she sat still for a few

moments, chewing on one arm of her glasses. Evelyne walked in with a stack of messages and set them on the desk.

"What are you grinning about?" she asked with a smile.

"Huh? Am I grinning?"

"Like a schoolgirl in love," Evelyne replied. "What's going on?"

"I have a date with my husband tonight."

Evelyne's eyes widened. "Really? Well, look at you. Are you two the cutest things?"

"I think we might be," Debbie replied with a laugh, her cheeks warming.

"If I ever get married, I want a marriage like that."

"You will. Don't give up."

Evelyne shrugged. "It's hard not to. I'm thirty-four years old. I'm supposed to be married with three kids by now. And online dating is the worst. I feel like I've been on a first date with every single man in his thirties in the entire city. And not one of them was marriage material."

Debbie sighed. "You are a wonderful person. I know you'll find him one day."

"I hope I find him before my eggs shrivel up and die," Evelyne said. "Oh, and your four-thirty appointment cancelled, so you're done for the day."

"Wonderful," Debbie replied. "I'm going home early to get ready for my date."

"Have fun," Evelyne said. "I want to hear all about it next week."

* * *

Debbie hurried home and had a long, luxurious bath with oils and candles. Then she blow-dried her hair and dressed in a long navy gown with a set of pearls her mother had given her.

When Caleb got home, she was ready to leave and had poured them each a small glass of scotch on ice.

She handed him the glass and took his briefcase. Then she kissed him softly. "Welcome home, honey."

"I could get used to this, you know? It's a dangerous precedent to set," he said as he took her in one arm and planted another, deeper kiss on her lips.

It was as though her breath was snatched from her lungs. She felt giddy. How long had it been since she'd responded to him this way? It felt like forever.

She sat and watched him dress while they chatted about their days and sipped their scotch. Then it was time to leave. They walked outside, and an Uber pulled up to the front of the building. They climbed in.

"Where are you taking me?" she asked.

"It's a surprise," he said.

She snuggled into his side, and he rested his arm around her shoulders. The city was brightly lit by now, with lights dotting the sides of skyrise buildings all around them. Traffic was heavy, with cars stopping and starting, the occasional honk and the rev of engines. He smelled like cologne and scotch. His arm around her was warm and heavy.

The car wove in and out of traffic, down one-way streets and through the city until they were in Fortitude Valley. The night was young; most of the foot traffic was still business related rather than party goers. But there were clumps of young people here and there. The girls, in skimpy clothing, clip-clopping in high platform shoes, and the boys standing about looking awkward in line outside nightclubs.

The Uber pulled up to the curb, and they stepped out.

"Where are we?" Debbie scanned the street, feeling suddenly very overdressed in the midst of the hip nightlife scene and the hurrying commuters on their way home from work after a long week.

"You don't know yet?" Caleb took her hand and led her down the footpath.

Suddenly it clicked. They'd come here on their very first date. He'd brought her to a small restaurant tucked away on a backstreet of the Valley, and they'd sat on cushions and eaten with their fingers. And it'd been incredible, romantic and delicious.

"Garuva?"

He laughed. "That's right. I hope you don't mind sitting on a cushion while we eat."

"I suppose I can do it one more time. Although you may have to help me back to my feet again."

He led the way to the narrow door. She wouldn't have spotted or recognised it if she'd been walking by. Inside, it was quite dark. The entire space was decorated with long, hanging curtains dividing cubicles with cushions on the floor. It was lit by candles, and hushed conversations radiated out to greet them.

They sat in one of the curtained squares on large cushions that were reasonably comfortable. Debbie adjusted her dress so she could sit cross-legged, then adjusted again when she found that wouldn't work for long.

They ate bites of shark dipped in a spicy sauce. Salt-and-pepper calamari breaded and fried. Various pastry-covered parcels like spring rolls, dumplings and samosa. And they finished with an assortment of sweet treats, including cheesecake and biscotti with coffee. It was a complete mish-mash of food styles and cuisines, and she loved every minute of it.

"Do you remember how young we were when we were here the first time?" Caleb asked as he sipped his coffee.

"I think I was twenty-seven, and you were twenty-nine."

"That sounds about right. I knew then..."

"Knew what?" she asked.

"That I was going to marry you and spend the rest of my life with you."

"It was our first date," she said with a laugh.

He nodded. "It was. But I knew. Right away."

Her face was warm from the wine and candlelight, but it felt warmer after his words. "You didn't have any hesitation?"

He smiled. "Nope. None. I never got cold feet or anything like that. I knew that you were the one, and that didn't change. It still hasn't changed. We got a bit off track for a while there. I felt unseen and hurt, and I know we're still working through some things. But I wanted you to understand that I haven't changed my perspective—we're meant for each other."

Tears filled her eyes. "Marriage is harder than I thought it'd be."

He nodded. "It is. Much harder."

"We always had such a great connection. I think we took it for granted and didn't work hard enough to keep it."

"I didn't know how," he said. "I'm sorry."

"Me too."

Chapter Thirty-Three

In Sunshine, it was the first date for Emily and Aaron. Emily was so nervous, she thought she might be sick. She hovered over the toilet, half-dressed. Then the feeling passed, and she continued dressing. She wore a pair of skinny jeans, a blush-coloured blouse and a pair of black leather flats.

She had no idea where Aaron might take her. Maybe she was underdressed. She should ask him where they were going. He was only in the next bedroom.

With her purse under her arm, she glanced in the bathroom mirror one last time. She'd curled her hair, and her makeup looked well done, if a little over the top. She always made her makeup too thick when she was nervous. Then she walked out the door and turned left to stand in front of Aaron's shut door. She was a little early. Maybe she should wait.

She raised her hand and knocked. Then waited. What was she doing? This was embarrassing. She should've stayed in her room so he could come looking for her. Wasn't that the right etiquette? She didn't know anymore. Times had changed, and she rarely dated. She turned to leave, and his door swung open. He wore a pair of jeans slung low around his hips. His muscular chest was bare.

"Oh, hey," he said. "I'm sorry. Am I running late?" He glanced at his watch.

"No, you're fine. I'm a little early. I wanted to ask if I'm dressed okay, or should I wear something else?"

He smiled. "You look perfect. I'll just throw on a shirt and some shoes, okay?"

She waited in the lounge room, her nerves abating a little as she drew several deep breaths. It was Aaron. She'd known him forever. They ate dinner together almost every night. But since he'd moved into Joanna's house, she'd gotten to know him in a way she'd never thought possible.

They talked about everything and nothing. They laughed together, watched TV together. She was comfortable around him, something she didn't think she'd ever be able to say about the high school bad boy who'd broken her heart all those years ago. They were friends. So why was she this nervous? Perhaps it was because she didn't want to do anything to jeopardise that friendship. He'd fast become one of the most important people in her life. Maybe the most important, if she was being completely honest.

She didn't have a lot of friends. And her family consisted of an extremely busy sister and her two small children. Everyone else lived so far away she rarely saw them. Joanna was her family now. And so was Aaron.

He drove her to a restaurant down by the water's edge. It was a small seafood place with a great view over the beach and ocean. It was dark, but the moon glistened golden in a straight line from the horizon to the beach. They sat outside surrounded by soft lighting. The sounds of the ocean were their backdrop.

"This is nice. I haven't eaten here in ages," Emily said.

Aaron handed her a menu. "I know... I remember when it opened. It was so exciting."

"There were hardly any restaurants on the island back then. Now we have dozens of them."

"Dozens?" He laughed. "I guess you're probably right. Although it still feels like such a tiny little community to me."

They ordered their meals and some drinks. Emily got a French martini for something different, and Aaron chose a boutique local beer. Then the dishes arrived. She had the salmon, while he'd ordered a pasta with a mix of seafood and a creamy sauce.

"Want to try it?" he asked.

"Only if you don't mind."

"Of course. Why don't we get an extra plate and we can share our meals?"

"Really?"

"Yeah, I like trying things. I'm sure you do too."

They got the waitress's attention and split their meals in half. Emily took a bite of the pasta and was immediately grateful.

"Do you like it?" he asked.

She nodded, still chewing. "It's delicious. Thank you. How was work today?"

"I'm starting to enjoy it. And some of the people are pretty nice."

"That's good. Do you miss the military?"

"Every day," he said. "But it was time for something new. Most of my mates had left already, and I was faced with starting again with an entirely new team or leaving."

"What was the deciding factor?" she asked, then took a bite of salmon. It was moist and hot, and had been caramelised in a soy-and-honey sauce.

"I was ready to settle down. I want to get married, have a

family. It's something I've always wanted. But now I think I'm ready for it. What about you?"

Her heart skipped a beat. He'd changed so much since high school, she almost didn't recognise him. Who was this man, talking about family and children? He wasn't the sullen and popular jock, always up to mischief of some kind or another, who she remembered. "Same for me. It's all I've ever wanted, really. I never much dreamed of a career. Only a family."

He reached for her hand. Squeezed it.

"Sometimes people think it's simple or not very ambitious. But I didn't have a close-knit family growing up. It was just me and my sister. My Dad left, my Mum worked a lot. And so Wanda and I kind of leaned on each other. And I used to say, *I can't wait to have a family of my own. Because I'm going to love them and be there for them, and finally have the homelife I needed but never got.*"

"That makes sense," he said. "I had good parents, so I'm pretty lucky that way."

"I'm scared to death I'll be just like my parents were when it comes down to it. But I'm going to do everything I can not to be."

"I can tell you'll be a good mother. It makes me happy to see Gran doing so well. And a lot of that is because of you."

Her heart swelled. "Thank you. That means so much to me. This job with her has meant the world. And I really do love it."

"I can tell," he said with a warm smile. "You're good at it. So, how many kids do you want?"

She grinned. "I want a bunch of them."

He laughed. "How many?"

"I don't know. Four or five."

"Five?"

She giggled. "Maybe four."

"Do they make cars that fit five kids?"

She shook her head. "I have no idea. I think so. Don't they have seven-seaters?"

"I guess that's true. Five kids. Wow."

"What about you?" she asked.

He smiled. "I love kids, so I'm open to having as many as possible."

After they finished dinner, they walked along the beach hand in hand and talked about their hopes, dreams and plans for the future. The more they spoke, the more relaxed Emily felt. He was the person she most wanted to see each day. The person she wanted to share her troubles and victories with. When she thought about the future, she couldn't imagine him not being in it. She hoped he felt the same way.

They ate gelato from a small place at the end of the beach, then wound their way back to the car on the footpath. Kids flew by on skateboards. Couples wandered between restaurants. The air was warm and smelled of salt and a mixture of foods.

When they got back to the house, Emily was giddy with happiness. It'd been a perfect romantic evening. Aaron knew just how to put her at ease. He'd made her feel special and yet relaxed. She was more herself with him than she'd ever been with anyone.

He stopped outside her bedroom. She turned to face him. "Thank you for a lovely evening."

"You're welcome," he said. He moved closer and raised a hand to cup her cheek.

Her heart thudded against her ribcage. Was he going to kiss her? The only other time he'd kissed her had been at the kissing booth when she was a teenager. Her very first kiss. But now he was a man. His cologne was intoxicating. The touch of his hand on her skin made it tingle. He was very close now, hovering over her, his lips just above hers.

Then he was kissing her. His second hand cupped her other cheek now. He pulled her closer to him, deepening the kiss. And her arms wound their way around his neck. She stood on tiptoe, her eyes shut, as she was swept up in the passion of it. Her whole world stood still. Nothing else mattered but him, their kiss and this moment.

Chapter Thirty-Four

They agreed to meet at a café to discuss their marriage. It was safer than at the house, where Gwen was certain her husband would launch into some kind of tirade, yell and lose his temper with her. She didn't want that. She'd had plenty of it over the years. And what they really needed to do was to get things out on the table between them, to discuss what'd happened to their relationship, and to figure out a way forward in a mature fashion.

Was it possible? She wasn't sure. But they owed it to themselves to try.

She arrived at the *Black Cat Café* ten minutes early. She wanted to have some time to prepare herself, to calm her nerves before he arrived. He'd been living at a motel, as far as she was aware. And she knew he wanted to come home. That was his goal, from what their phone calls had told her. But she'd assured him that wasn't going to happen and he needed to find a more permanent place to stay.

He still believed he could save their relationship, but she wasn't sure why he wanted to, given she'd had several locals report back to her that his girlfriend continued to visit him at the motel and she had even stayed over several nights. Now that everyone knew they were separated, it was amazing how many of them had known about his affair but had never said anything to her before now. They were all coming out of the woodwork with their stories and commiserations.

She would force a smile on her face as she listened, but all she could think was, why didn't they tell her sooner? Why did no one say anything? They'd spotted him kissing and cuddling his girlfriend at the gym, at restaurants, even behind the church in the parking lot. But no one thought it was their place to say anything to Gwen until now.

It made her angrier than she could express. But she held it in because it did no one any good for her to lose her cool. It'd probably justify in their minds why he felt the need to have an affair, with such a nagging wife. Even though she'd been acquainted with most of them for decades, and they should've known better.

She ordered herself a cappuccino and an apple cinnamon muffin and was browsing the news headlines on her phone when Duncan arrived. He sat across from her with a scowl. His face dripped sweat, and he set a bicycle helmet on the ground by his feet.

"Thanks for letting me come into my own garage to get my bike," he said. "It was really thoughtful of you."

"Good morning, Duncan," she said with a bright smile. "You seem to be in a lovely mood."

"I'm living in a motel, Gwen. The bed is giving me chronic back pain. And the food has caused constant indigestion and heartburn."

"I'm sorry to hear that." She was sorry. She didn't want him to be uncomfortable or unhappy. Well, maybe a little bit.

"Let me come home. Please, I'm begging you. I miss your

cooking, our bed, the lounge room. Well, all of it. It's my house too. You can't just kick me out of my own home."

She sighed. It was hard to see him like this. She'd loved him for such a long time, and she was used to giving in to his demands. He was such a bulldozer and she was a people pleaser, so she'd always done whatever he wanted. That way, she didn't suffer his temper tantrums, and life could be smooth. He was used to her giving in, and she could see on his face that he expected her to cave.

"I'm sorry, Duncan. I don't want you back at the house. We need to talk through what's going on in our marriage and how to deal with everything moving forward. Let's focus on that. Okay? And as I said to you the last time we spoke about it, maybe you should look for a flat to rent. That way, you can buy yourself a good mattress and make some home-cooked food to eat."

He gaped at her. "Cook for myself?"

"Yes, Duncan. Cook for yourself. You're a very capable man—I'm sure you can read a recipe and follow the instructions."

His face turned red. "I'm a busy man. I don't have time for all that. I've got work and the gym..."

"Yes, I know all about it, Duncan."

"But you don't care? Clearly you've already written us off. We made vows, Gwen."

This wasn't going the way she'd hoped. She didn't want him to get so worked up. If he did, they'd never make it through the list of subjects she wanted to discuss.

"Duncan, I want us to be honest with one another. Can you do that?"

He grunted then nodded.

"Okay, great. Do you still love me?"

He frowned. "Of course I do."

"I mean, really love me. Not like, you love me because I'm in your family and have always been there for you. But are you in love with me?"

He shrugged. "I don't know. What does that even mean?"

"I think you've answered that, then," she said as her heart squeezed. "I love you, but I can't be in a relationship with someone who doesn't love me back. It's not fair on me, or you, really. If you love this other person, you should be with her. I have no desire to stand in the way of that. You've betrayed our marriage vows, and you've betrayed me and my commitment to us."

He leaned forward. "And I'm sorry for that. I really am. I don't want our marriage to be over."

"But it is, honey." She patted his hand. "I don't want that either, but you ended it the moment you started an affair. And from what I hear, the affair is still well and truly underway."

He blanched. "Who told you that?"

"Everyone. The entire island has been watching you, apparently for quite a while. They just failed to inform me of the affair until now. And suddenly it's like a news super-highway around here."

He groaned and rubbed his hands over his face. "Busybodies!"

"Why do you want to stay married, Duncan? If you'd rather be with her, what's the point of our marriage continuing?"

"We were going to grow old together. I like having you around. I like our home. It's nice."

"I'm afraid that's not enough for me," she said. "You like how I take care of you and our home. But there's more to me than that. I'm a person, a whole person. And I deserve to have someone love and respect me enough to be faithful and to put effort into our relationship."

He sighed. "Okay. So, what now?"

"I need you to move your things out of the house and find a place to live. We can talk to divorce solicitors if you want, but I think we can probably negotiate a settlement without them. I'd like to sell the house and get a small flat by the beach, I think. I'll be travelling a lot, so I won't need much to maintain here."

"What? Sell the house?" His eyes widened. "But that's our home, where we raised our family."

"I know, but it's time to put that all behind us and embrace the next phase of life."

"You're so callous sometimes, Gwen. I don't understand it."

"I'm not callous, honey. I'm all cried out."

When she got home, she found that she wasn't all cried out. And she spent the next hour lying on the couch with tears trailing down her cheeks and wetting the fabric. She didn't want to sell her home, but it was far too big for her to manage on her own. And it was time to put the memories of the past behind her. Everything reminded her of Duncan. His selfishness, his preference for dark and moody furniture and lighting, his dominance in every area of their lives. She'd wanted a light, airy home.

He'd refused everything she ever wanted, and she'd let him get away with his controlling behaviour for decades because she loved him and she wanted him to be happy. Now she could see how badly that had backfired. He was a selfish man who didn't consider her feelings one bit when he decided to look elsewhere for some comfort. She would sell it all and decorate her own flat with modern decor.

Brandon's car pulled into the driveway. She wiped her face

dry with a tissue and then answered the door with as big a smile as she could manage.

"Oh, Mum," he said when he saw her face.

The grandkids all looked at her with big, wide eyes, clearly worried as to why Nanna was crying. She must've looked a fright.

"Go inside and check the cookie jar," she said. "I bought you all a special treat."

With a grin, they ran inside and shouted for joy in the kitchen over the Wagon Wheels they found in the jar—chocolate-covered cookies with a marshmallow and jam centre.

Brandon embraced her, and she let her head rest on his shoulder for several minutes. Then he released her and kissed the top of her head. Gwen shut the door behind them and sat in the front room with him.

"Dad told me you want a divorce," he said.

She nodded. "I'm sorry, honey."

"It's okay. I get it. If Mara cheated on me, I'd die."

"You wouldn't die," Gwen replied. "But you'd feel like you had."

Brandon rested a hand on her leg. "I'm sorry, Mum. That's not fair on you. You've always put this family first and given so much of yourself over the years. He's been a self-centred, arrogant jerk my whole life. You didn't deserve this."

"Thank you for saying that," Gwen replied, feeling choked up all over again. "It means a lot to me."

"I love him, of course. But he shouldn't have treated you this way, and I told him so."

"Thanks, honey. I need your support right now. I'm not sure I can make it without you kids."

"Well, you have us. I've spoken to the others, and we're all going to be here for you far more than we have been. We all agreed that we took you for granted, and for far too long, we've followed Dad's lead in how we treated you. But that's all going to change."

"Really? That is music to my ears," she said as tears fell once again. "I love you all so much. I want you to be happy, and so I do whatever I can to make sure that happens. But I think I've spoiled you a little too often."

He laughed. "Yes, you have. But we appreciate you. It isn't unseen, Mum. Even if sometimes we act that way."

Chapter Thirty-Five

Five months later, it was July, and the weather had turned cool. As cool as it would ever get in Sunshine, which made it absolutely perfect. The sun was shining, the sky was a deeper blue than it had been in summer, and the sun sparkled off the surface of the ocean.

Joanna set her hands on her hips to take in the view. Then with a long inhale and a wide smile, she returned to the house to finish preparing for their potluck brunch. The theme today was Spanish tapas, and she'd had a lot of fun devising the menu and cooking the food. She hoped everyone would enjoy it. Emily had gone overboard on the desserts. They would all be rolling out of the dining room later, but that's how it always was for one of their brunches.

Inside, Gwen was putting the finishing touches on the decor. The boot was long gone and she looked positively radiant in a pair of jeans with brown boots and a white cardigan. She'd chosen to decorate with warm colours—shades of red, orange, yellow. There were swathes of fabric hung over the backs of each chair in alternating colours. A vase of red flowers stood in the centre of the table. She'd even painted several canvases with slashes of deep red and orange and set them on the sideboard against the wall behind the table.

"It looks so good in here," Joanna said. "You've outdone yourself again."

"Thanks, honey. The food smells divine. Also, I brought some chocolate to go with our coffee after dessert."

"That's perfect," Joanna replied. "We have plenty. We're waiting on Debbie, and then we can get started. I'll find some music to play on the sound system."

As she returned to the hallway, Aaron walked out, pulling a rolling suitcase behind him. She paused to allow him to make his way into the kitchen, then followed. A lump formed in her throat. She didn't want him to move out yet. It seemed as though he'd only recently arrived. But time had flown, and he'd chosen to purchase a townhouse closer to the city so his commute wouldn't be so long. He was moving out today after the brunch. It would be the last one he shared with them, at least until he next visited.

"I'm going to miss you, sweetheart," Joanna said, reaching up to give him another hug. She'd hugged him three times already that morning. It would never be enough.

He laughed. "I'll visit, Gran. I promise."

"You'd better. And maybe I'll come and see your new place once you're settled. Would that be okay?"

"It would be awesome," he replied.

"I'll bring you food."

"Even better." He grinned. "Emily will be coming over, and I'll be here to visit her as well. We'll see each other a lot."

Aaron and Emily had been very close lately. Since their first date, they'd spent more and more time together. It seemed to Joanna that things between them were becoming serious. She hoped, for both their sakes, that it would all work out. They were very sweet together and perfect for one another, in her opinion.

"Speaking of food... I'm going to have to leave early. I won't make it for your brunch. Sorry, Gran. But I have to meet the real estate agent to get the keys, and she's busy later."

"Oh, dear," Joanna said. "That's a shame. Never mind. I'll pack you a plate to take with you."

"I won't have a fridge to put it in for a while, so instead why don't you just feed me the next time I visit and we'll call it even?" He winked.

She laughed at that. "Okay, I suppose I can live with that. Here—you can take this bread roll at least or you'll starve."

"Thanks, Gran. I can't ever starve with you around."

"No one is starving with Joanna around," Emily agreed as she pulled a tray of garlic-stuffed mushroom caps from the oven. "I think I've gained about ten kilograms living here."

She set the mushrooms on the kitchen bench, and Aaron grabbed her around the waist, pulling her to his chest with a laugh. "You look perfect to me."

She kissed him on the lips. Joanna beamed at the two of them. "You're adorable. But give me another hug before you go, honey. I'm going to miss you so much."

Aaron extricated himself to kiss Joanna on the cheek. Then she waved him goodbye from the front door. Emily walked out to the car with him.

Joanna returned to the kitchen to plate up the food. There was garlic shrimp and spicy chorizo. Crispy calamari served with marina sauce. Golden, crunchy empanadillas gallegas filled with tuna, egg and chopped olives. And corn muffins with whipped garlic butter.

The front door opened as she was finishing up, and Debbie stepped in carrying a tray in her hands. "Hello, my lovelies! What's this box?"

"Box? What do you mean?" Joanna replied.

"There's a big box at your front door. Right in the way."

"Oh? I didn't see it."

Joanna hurried around to look, wiping her hands on the floral apron tied neatly around her waist. She kissed Debbie on the cheek, then studied the box that almost entirely blocked the front door. "Let's see." She read the label on the top of it, and her heart leapt. "It's our book! Our book is here. Quick, help me get this box inside the house."

Debbie placed her platter on the bench. "By the way, there's a lot of kissing going on at the end of your driveway. I blushed as I walked by."

Joanna chuckled as the two of them pushed the box into the house. It was too heavy to lift. She had to shove it at the same time as Debbie, and it took them a minute or two to get it over the threshold. Finally, it was inside, and they were both huffing. They pushed it to the kitchen table and collapsed into two chairs with a grunt.

"It's very heavy," Debbie said.

"I wonder why they didn't ring the doorbell."

"They never do anymore," Debbie replied.

Gwen walked into the kitchen. "Debbie, you're here! We're ready to go as soon as you are. I'm famished."

"Our book is here!" Joanna said, feeling a wobble in her voice. She was so excited about this recipe book—it'd been written with her best friends in all the world. Something she never thought would be possible, but that she'd always wanted.

Gwen's face lit up. "Oh, goody. Let's open it and take a look." She brought over a pair of scissors she found in a kitchen drawer. "Should we wait for Emily?"

Joanna frowned. "Maybe we should... but I'm sure she won't mind if we have a little look first."

She cut the box open and pulled out a book to hand to each of them. Then she held one herself, turning it over and flipping through the pages. The front cover had a photograph of all four of them seated on the front steps of Joanna's house.

The flowers were in full bloom around them, and they were each holding a plate of food and laughing about something scandalous Debbie had just told them. She recalled the moment fondly with a smile on her face.

"It looks amazing," Joanna said in a soft voice.

Debbie and Gwen both exchanged a glance with Joanna, their eyes glistening.

"I can't believe this," Gwen said.

"It's everything I hoped," Debbie added.

Just then, Emily returned to the house with red eyes. She fetched some tissues from the kitchen and blew her nose. Then she turned her attention to the ladies who were all watching her.

"What?"

"Are you okay, honey?" Joanna asked.

Emily nodded, tearing up again. "He's not going far."

"You'll see him all the time," Gwen added.

"Absence makes the heart grow fonder...or something like that," Debbie said.

They all laughed.

Emily rolled her eyes. "Thanks, Deb."

"Come and see this," Joanna said. "Our book is here."

Emily joined them, soon smiling again, her tears forgotten.

After they'd looked through every page and laughed and cried together over how well it had worked—far better than any of them imagined it could—they sat around the table and raised glasses of sangria high overhead.

"To all of you, my Potluck Society friends," Joanna said.

"Friends for life," Gwen added with a sniffle.

"Friends for life!" Debbie and Emily agreed.

They clinked the glasses together as each shouted, "Cheers!"

The food was delicious. Joanna especially liked the mushroom cups. And the sangria was divine, fruity and strong with a healthy serving of ice, just the way she liked it.

"How are things with you?" she asked Gwen as she reached for a corn muffin.

Gwen sighed. "I filed for divorce."

"Really? Are you sure?" Debbie asked.

Gwen nodded. "I'm sure. We've been seeing a therapist, trying to work things out. But my heart wasn't in it. I can't trust him again, and I don't believe he loves me. Not the way I need or want to be loved. I don't want to live the rest of my life with a man who doesn't care about me—I've wasted enough years doing that."

"How do the children feel about it?" Emily asked.

"They understand. It's taken a while for all of them to come around, but they get it now."

Joanna left to get the dessert from the kitchen. Emily came with her to make coffee. There were tiny magdalenas, little cakes dusted with icing sugar, and cinnamon and orange crema catalana, similar to creme brûlée. The cappuccinos would go nicely with the desserts and help to cut the sweetness. She also carried Gwen's chocolates on a tray with the rest of the dishes.

"Dessert is coming up!" she declared as she carried it all into the dining room and set it on the serving board.

"You shouldn't have done so much hard work, Jo. You're spoiling us," Gwen said.

"I love it—you know that. Besides, Emily does a lot of the heavy lifting these days. She's becoming quite the cook."

Emily's cheeks flushed pink as she handed around cappuccinos. "Thanks, Jo. You're a good teacher."

"What did I miss?" Joanna asked as she returned to her seat.

"Gwen was saying she's had an offer on the house and has found a lovely unit by the beach."

"Oh, good for you," Joanna replied. "That sounds perfect."

"Duncan was upset about it, but he didn't offer to buy the place because he knows he'd have to maintain it on his own. He liked it when I cleaned and cooked for him but isn't a fan of doing those things himself."

"Of course," Debbie replied with an eye roll. "Never mind, it's not your job any longer. Maybe his girlfriend will take care of him."

"I doubt that," Gwen replied. "She broke up with him a few weeks ago."

"No!" Joanna said. "Really? Wow. That's got to be a bit of a wake-up call for him."

"It was," Gwen said. "He begged pretty hard for me to take him back after that happened. He even cried and said he'd made a huge mistake. But I can't trust him. As I said, he broke my heart, and I'm not sure it'll ever be mended."

Joanna patted her hand. "You'll find your joy again. I know you will."

"Maybe, but it will take a while. I'm not sure I'll ever trust someone again, though."

Joanna didn't respond to that. She hoped her friend would learn to love again, but now wasn't the time to say that. She would be there for her and support her, and that was what Gwen needed.

"How are things with you, Deb?" Gwen asked. Clearly she wanted to change the subject, but Joanna was happy to let her.

"I'm fine," Debbie replied.

"We're going to need a little more detail than that," Emily said as she dug into her crema catalana.

Debbie's lips pursed for a moment. "I don't want to rub anyone's nose…"

Gwen frowned. "Are you saying you don't want to talk

about how happy you are because I'm miserable and going through a hard time?"

Debbie swallowed.

Gwen shook her head. "Debbie Holmes! I hope you know that you can always share happy times with me. It won't upset me. It actually helps me to be happy. Gives me hope as well that maybe I'll be there someday."

Debbie nodded. "Okay. I'm glad. I want you to be happy. And things with Caleb are going so well. We're closer than we've ever been. We're headed to Venice for our anniversary, and we're going to have a romantic gondola ride, and visit museums and art galleries and see this amazing choir at St Mark's Cathedral. I'm really looking forward to it."

"That sounds fantastic and so romantic," Emily said, her eyes gleaming.

"Good for you, honey," Joanna said.

"Yes, I'm happy for you both," Gwen added. "So happy. I want you to thrive in your relationship. At least someone is getting that."

She stood to her feet and went to give Debbie a hug. Debbie stood too and laced her arms around Gwen's petite frame. Then Joanna decided to join them, and finally Emily hurried around the table too. All four women stood in an embrace, giggling and trying not to lose their balance. Tears filled Joanna's eyes as she felt the warmth and love in that hug. These were friendships that had stood the test of time—women who wanted the best for her, who'd been there for her through the hard times and celebrated with her in the good times. They'd all experienced a year of change, of growth and of sorrow, of loss and of achievement. And she couldn't wait to see what came next for the four of them in the years ahead.

* * *

Thank you for reading **The Sunshine Potluck Society**! *I hope you enjoyed visiting Sunshine, Bribie Island. And if you'd like to visit with Joanna, Debbie, Gwen & Emily again, you can order the next book in the series,* **Sunshine Reservations** *now.*
   Return to Sunshine with Book 2...

"**Love, love, love** these books!" ⭐⭐⭐⭐⭐

Want to find out about all of my new releases? Click here to be notified about new stories when you download this free book!
   Keep scrolling to find out about all of my other books.
   If you'd like to join my Facebook reader group, where we talk about what we're reading and have other fun together, you can do that here.

Also by Lilly Mirren

WOMEN'S FICTION

CORAL ISLAND SERIES

The Island

After twenty five years of marriage and decades caring for her two children, on the evening of their vow renewal, her husband shocks her with the news that he's leaving her.

The Beach Cottage

Beatrice is speechless. It's something she never expected — a secret daughter. She and Aidan have only just renewed their romance, after decades apart, and he never mentioned a child. Did he know she existed?

The Blue Shoal Inn

Taya's inn is in trouble. Her father has built a fancy new resort in Blue Shoal and hired a handsome stranger to manage it. When the stranger offers to buy her inn and merge it with the resort, she wants to hate him but when he rescues a stray dog her feelings for him change.

Island Weddings

Charmaine moves to Coral Island and lands a job working at a local florist shop. It seems as though the entire island has caught wedding fever, with weddings planned every weekend. It's a good opportunity for her to get to know the locals, but what she doesn't expect is to be thrown into the middle of a family drama.

The Island Bookshop

Evie's book club friends are the people in the world she relies on most. But when one of the newer members finds herself confronted with her past, the rest of the club will do what they can to help, endangering the existence of the bookshop without realising it.

An Island Reunion

It's been thirty five years since the friends graduated from Coral Island State Primary School and the class is returning to the island to celebrate.

THE WARATAH INN SERIES

The Waratah Inn

Wrested back to Cabarita Beach by her grandmother's sudden death, Kate Summer discovers a mystery buried in the past that changes everything.

One Summer in Italy

Reeda leaves the Waratah Inn and returns to Sydney, her husband, and her thriving interior design business, only to find her marriage in tatters. She's lost sight of what she wants in life and can't recognise the person she's become.

The Summer Sisters

Set against the golden sands and crystal clear waters of Cabarita Beach three sisters inherit an inn and discover a mystery about their grandmother's past that changes everything they thought they knew about their family...

Christmas at The Waratah Inn

Liz Cranwell is divorced and alone at Christmas. When her friends convince her to holiday at The Waratah Inn, she's dreading her first Christmas on her own. Instead she discovers that strangers can be the balm to heal the wounds of a lonely heart in this heartwarming Christmas story.

EMERALD COVE SERIES

Cottage on Oceanview Lane

When a renowned book editor returns to her roots, she rediscovers her strength & her passion in this heartwarming novel.

Seaside Manor Bed & Breakfast

The Seaside Manor Bed and Breakfast has been an institution in Emerald Cove for as long as anyone can remember. But things are changing and Diana is nervous about what the future might hold for her and her husband, not to mention the historic business.

Bungalow on Pelican Way

Moving to the Cove gave Rebecca De Vries a place to hide from her abusive ex. Now that he's in jail, she can get back to living her life as a police officer in her adopted hometown working alongside her intractable but very attractive boss, Franklin.

Chalet on Cliffside Drive

At forty-four years of age, Ben Silver thought he'd never find love. When he moves to Emerald Cove, he does it to support his birth mother, Diana, after her husband's sudden death. But then he meets Vicky.

An Emerald Cove Christmas

The Flannigan family has been through a lot together. They've grown and changed over the years and now have a blended and extended family that doesn't always see eye to eye. But this Christmas they'll learn that love can overcome all of the pain and differences of the past in this inspiring Christmas tale.

MYSTERIES

White Picket Lies

Fighting the demons of her past Toni finds herself in the midst of a second marriage breakdown at forty seven years of age. She struggles to keep depression at bay while doing her best to raise a wayward teenaged son and uncover the identity of the killer.

In this small town investigation, it's only a matter of time until friends and neighbours turn on each other.

HISTORICAL FICTION (WRITING AS BRONWEN PRATLEY)

Beyond the Crushing Waves

An emotional standalone historical saga. Two children plucked from poverty & forcibly deported from the UK to

Australia. Inspired by true events. An unforgettable tale of loss, love, redemption & new beginnings.

Under a Sunburnt Sky

Inspired by a true story. Jan Kostanski is a normal Catholic boy in Warsaw when the nazis invade. He's separated from his neighbours, a Jewish family who he considers kin, by the ghetto wall. Jan and his mother decide that they will do whatever it takes to save their Jewish friends from certain death. The unforgettable tale of an everyday family's fight against evil, and the unbreakable bonds of their love.

About the Author

Lilly Mirren is an Amazon top 20, Audible top 15 and *USA Today* Bestselling author who has sold over two million copies of her books worldwide. She lives in Brisbane, Australia with her husband and three children.

Her books combine heartwarming storylines with realistic characters readers see as friends.

Her debut series, *The Waratah Inn*, set in the delightful Cabarita Beach, hit the *USA Today* Bestseller list and since then, has touched the hearts of hundreds of thousands of readers across the globe.

Made in the USA
Middletown, DE
12 September 2024